The Spirited Ladies of Liberty Street

a story of Liberation and Liquor in Prohibition

Pat Dodd Helen Chantal Pike

Outskirts Press, Inc.
Denver, Colorado

This is a work of fiction. The events and characters described herein are imaginary and are not intended to refer to specific places or living persons. The opinions expressed in this manuscript are solely the opinions of the author and do not represent the opinions or thoughts of the publisher. The author has represented and warranted full ownership and/or legal right to publish all the materials in this book.

The Spirited Ladies of Liberty Street
A Story of Liberation and Liquor in Prohibition

V3.0

Outskirts Press, Inc.
http://www.outskirtspress.com

ISBN: 978-1-4327-4073-3

Library of Congress Control Number: 2009928881

PRINTED IN THE UNITED STATES OF AMERICA

Dedication

The Spirited Ladies of Liberty Street is dedicated to Bunny Dodd Monteverdi, my sister, whose help and encouragement since the beginning made this book possible. As your big brother, I will love you forever.

Acknowledgements

The journey through years of research was made enjoyable thanks to the assistance of several notable individuals who are no longer here to share in the fruits of our labor. I would like to recognize the support I received from my late brother-in-law, John 'Skip' Monteverdi, Florence Valore Miller of Atlantic City, Bennett Herman, City of Orange historian, and Ray Reitman, owner of Galsworthy Wholesale Liquors.

Many thanks go to Marvin Soloman for sharing recollections of his father; Dan Hennigan from his days at the *Atlantic City Press;* Bob Ruffalo, historian and owner of Princeton Antiques and Books in Atlantic City; the White family, owners of the storied Marlborough Blenheim Hotel; the Sisters of Charity at St. John's Parish in Orange; Lisa Laird, ninth generation in her family to operate Laird & Company of Colts Neck and who graciously gave of her time to answer my many questions and to take me on a tour of the apple-jack distillery; Ray Foley, who began his career at The Manor in West Orange, and is now editor and publisher of *Bartender* magazine and author of several nationally recognized books on the craft of mixing a good drink, and to Lynn DeBlat who assisted me with transcribing, typing, editing, and proofreading this manuscript in its early stages.

A special nod of appreciation to Liz Reich for her patience as I worked on my first book.

I would also like to thank Bob Deerin, a columnist for *The Coaster* newspaper in Asbury Park. He saw fit to introduce me to fellow journalist, and author, Helen Pike. I outlined my story, showed her my notes, research and photographs, and sought her collaboration to turn the Dodds' more spirited tales into a book worthy of publication.

Together we would like to thank Julie Gannon of GoGannon Designs in Ocean Grove for the colorful cover that wraps this historical narrative.

We'd also like to thank Raffaie Nahar who generously copy edited this manuscript even as he balanced his duties for Dow Jones in Singapore. Helen would also like to recognize Wayne Tiedemann and his parents Muriel and Herb, Joan Culloo McLaughlin Flatley and John Firestone, Esq. for their enthusiastic support.

Author's Foreword

I write this story, not only as a labor of love, but to leave my nephews and nieces, and their many children, a true, if somewhat glorified, story of their maternal ancestor, Kitty Kelleher Dodd. She took risks to break the cycle of poverty that faced her three children in order to give them a better start. I am the grateful recipient as her decisions ultimately gave me a life-long career in the hospitality industry.

Kitty, and my grandfather, John Dodd, are the only people in my story I didn't know. I was born in the family home in 1938, five years after my grandmother died. I grew up knowing the people on Liberty Street and later when the Dodds moved to Orange, the old families remained close friends. Bunny and I called most of Kitty's cohorts, aunts and their husbands, uncles. Their children were our playmates, and many of them are still our friends to this day.

After twelve o'clock Sunday mass at St. John's, the Dodds and Ryans would gather at the "big" house on Ridge Street for lunch. In fair weather they would eat and drink, sitting on wicker rocking chairs and settees on the large front porch, and reminisce. Rewarded with tips, Bunny and I would serve snacks. I would fetch drinks. At the age of seven, I could shake a whiskey sour or a Tom Collins and muddle a perfect Old Fashioned.

On special occasions, our cousin Doris, who was about twenty years older than me, would pass around her autograph book to the *oohs* and *aahs* of all. At other times, we'd linger over black-and-white photographs in a large leather-bound album that usually sat on the coffee table in the living room. A gold inscription on the cover read *With compliments and thanks from the White Family and Staff of the Marlborough Blenheim Hotel.* The album was filled with pictures taken during the family's vacation in Atlantic City.

The common denominator in all the tales from the past was Kitty Dodd, and many a toast was made in her memory. At a holiday dinner at my home, a decade or so after Uncle Jim died, Doris, then in her eighties, told me, Bunny, and her four children – Jay, Peter, Brian, and Annie – what her father hadn't divulged about living on Liberty Street during Prohibition.

Literary License

As I wanted to include some of my closest friends and professional associates in this literary adventure, with their written permission, I transported them back to the Roaring Twenties. Because the borders among all the Oranges are so porous, Helen and I let that single word represent all the municipalities. Following in another footstep of literary tradition, we hope you enjoy meeting the era's celebrities we have introduced into our historical narrative.

Among the repositories consulted for *The Spirited Ladies of Liberty Street: A Story of Liquor, Liberation and Prohibition* were the Orange Public Library; Alexander Library at Rutgers University, New Brunswick; New Jersey State Library, Trenton; New Jersey State Historical Society, Newark, and the U.S. Library of Congress.

Further information came from the Essex County Hall of Records; the archive at the Edison National Historic Site, West Orange; the U.S. Treasury Department; the National Guard Militia Museum of New Jersey, Sea Girt; historical records kept by the New Jersey State Police, U.S. Coast Guard and U. S. Treasury Department, and the Atlantic City Convention & Visitors Authority.

Critic Samuel Johnson wrote, "The greatest part of a writer's time is spent in reading in order to write. A man will turn over half a library to make a book." I learned how true those words were as I assembled material on the liquor industry, Prohibition, and organized crime for more than five years. The sophisticated Art Deco era especially caught my eye: geometric forms, tailored clothing, luxurious materials. Boy, would I have loved to have lived back then! And to have had a beer with Kitty!!

Prologue

Around noon on a cold wintry day, I got a phone call from Uncle Jim. In a concerned tone he said he would pick me up in a few minutes outside my district office. It was 1966, and I had recently been elected to the New Jersey State Legislature at the age of 28. I responded that I was very busy.

Protective of me and Bunny since our parents' death while we were still teenagers, my aunt's husband pressed the issue a second time. "It's important." By his tone and uncharacteristic seriousness, I knew whatever the matter was, it was not only significant but, in all likelihood, it was not good.

After we had driven a while through the streets of Orange, Uncle Jim spoke. "I received a call this morning from a John Patrick. He told me he found something he thinks belongs to the Dodd family. He knew I was your uncle, but he wants to return it to you personally."

I was still didn't understand Uncle Jim's dark mood, yet I sensed something was wrong. "Why the concern?"

"Because whatever he found, he found in a wall of the house

he and his wife just moved into," said Uncle Jim, "and that house is located at 37 Liberty Street, West Orange, the house you were born in."

Suddenly, all the stories from long ago when the Dodds and Ryans sat on the porch on Ridge Street began to take on an ominous cast.

"He doesn't want to return my lost baby rattle, I take it?"

Speaking more to himself than to me, Uncle Jim muttered, "Christ, we cleaned that house and grounds in detail, all of us. I can't think of anything we could have missed."

I cut in. "Uncle Jim, though you, nor the family ever told me, I know what went on there. Hell, it seems everyone but me knew. Whatever he found, the statute of limitations on bootlegging has long since run out."

My wise old uncle looked at me and softly smiled.

"Pat, you were just elected to a high state office. You're in a rough game now, politics. Anything could be used against you in the next election. This John Patrick knows you own several bars. He knows you have money. This could be a shakedown!"

We pulled up to the curb in front of 37 Liberty Street, climbed out of the car and walked up the steps. Mr. Patrick answered the door and introduced himself. Then he showed us into the kitchen. The rear wall of the room was half demolished and there were wallboard pieces lying around.

As he led us around to the other side, he explained that while waiting to get a job he had applied for, he and his wife agreed to open the kitchen by taking out this wall. He pointed to a line of wooden cabinets that were now all opened and empty. He explained how he uncovered them that morning. Then he led us back into the kitchen and pointed at two large canvas bags lying on top of a table.

"Ever since we moved in, people have told my wife and me

about the Dodd family," Mr. Patrick said. "The old families still living on the street talk about your grandmother, Kitty Dodd, and the wonderful things she did for so many people.

"I didn't know what else to do with what I came across but to give it to you," he added, pointing to the bags.

Just as Uncle Jim instructed, neither of us had said a word other than the greeting at the door. I looked at him now and he gave a slight shake of the head and unbuttoned his suit coat, revealing a .38 caliber Smith & Wesson police special in his pants' belt.

As I looked in the bag nearest me, I saw open packets loosely wrapped in heavy, plain brown paper. The first stack held fifty federal excise tax stamps from the U.S. Treasury Department that looked like the red tax stamps gracing the tops of all the liquor bottles I saw every day in my bars.

The next stack of fifties was the green excise tax stamps from Canada that would have been crisscrossed with the U.S. stamp on Canadian Club and Seagram's VO bottles. The third stack was blue tax stamps from Great Britain for bottles of Gilbey's London Dry Gin, Beefeaters, and all the Scotch bottles.

Uncle Jim and I then switched bags. In his were similar wrappers that held the distinctive cursive writing against a white background that made up the labels for Canadian Club whiskey. There was another set of red-and-white labels for Gilbey's Gin.

My look of amazement contrasted with Uncle Jim's dour disapproval as he slowly shook his head, mumbling to himself as he finished his inventory. Stepping back from the table, he broke the silence and looked at John Patrick. In a not-too-friendly voice, with his coat still opened to reveal the butt of the .38, he asked, "Did you find anything else? Is this all of it?"

In a hesitant voice, Mr. Patrick replied, "No, honest, that's everything."

"I don't know what all this stuff is, but I'll be glad to get rid of it for you Mr. Patrick," said Uncle Jim, masking his success as a top salesman for Galsworthy Liquor Distributors in Newark. "And what can we do for you?"

"No, honest. This is not what you think," Mr. Patrick said in a rush of words. "From all I've heard, you're good people. I don't want anything. I'm not even sure what it's all about. And, I don't want to know."

Looking at him, Uncle Jim and I sensed he was being genuine.

"To tell the truth, if it was cash I had found, I never would have called you!"

What a relief! This wasn't a shakedown.

Mr. Patrick's final outburst broke the tension and he proceeded to show us the house where my story begins. As we were leaving, I asked where he was looking for work. He said about a month ago he had put in a job application to be a driver for the Rheingold Brewery in Orange, but hadn't heard back.

We thanked him and left. On the drive back to my office, I asked my uncle, "What are you going to do with what's left of the afternoon?"

"After I put these bags in my apartment house's incinerator, I think I'll be ready for a drink, or two, or three!" he replied with a lopsided grin.

Deciding to save a memento from an untold chapter of Dodd family history, I took one example of each stamp and label from both bags before leaving Uncle Jim's car. We agreed to meet an hour later at Ernest and Werner's, a German-American restaurant on Main Street in West Orange. Back in my office, I called Tommy Quinn, the goodwill ambassador for Rheingold Brewery and asked him to look into John Patrick's application. I would appreciate any effort made on his behalf.

A half hour later, I drove back to Liberty Street. Just as I was placing a case of premium liquor on his front porch with a "thank you" envelope, Mr. Patrick threw open the front door and exclaimed, "This is my lucky day. I just got a call from Mr. Quinn, a vice president at Rheingold, saying I can start work tomorrow!"

A short time later I found Uncle Jim at the bar as he was ordering his usual Canadian Club and ginger highball. I took the stool next to him and ordered a Rheingold beer. As the afternoon melted into evening and we repaired to a private alcove table to eat, Uncle Jim told me the family story. Until the day he died, whenever we were alone, I'd ask him questions and he'd answer them. He seemed relieved to be able finally to tell the secret he had kept from more than thirty years ago, and I remain grateful to this day that he did!

Chapter 1:
End of summer, 1919

For one moment the night stood still. All was quiet outside the house. The three women left inside the modest two-story wood-frame home on Liberty Street made no sound of their own. Filtering through the front bedroom's thin white curtain, the moonlight brushed past an ink sketch of a harbor scene before finding Kitty Dodd who lay awake and alone. In another moment feelings she had willed away would rush in, linking fear about an uncertain future with the feelings of deprivation long buried when she'd left Ireland to come to America.

Two deaths tunneled her protected heart, one fresh and the other renewing the sorrow of her first loss. Born in a new country from the passion of a young marriage, Kitty's first-born, Mariah, was killed two years ago when a draft horse crashed through the windshield of her beau's new motor car on Eagle Rock Reservation in the Oranges. The crack to Mariah's skull and the swelling of her brain never gave Kitty's bright, independent older daughter a chance of survival. The doctors at Newark German Hospital, where Mariah was a maternity nurse, could do nothing to save her. Mariah's brothers buried their beloved older Sis on a cloudy September day and then, because their military draft numbers had been called, left to go to war.

Now, in short-lived triumph, they returned in time to bury their father. Kitty knew the man who shared her dreams of political and financial freedom, had loved to tipple. So had her own father. Even she enjoyed a celebratory nip now and again. But holding on to the promise of a new beginning in a new country, Kitty overlooked the drinking that grew as each child was born and money became scarcer. Rent from their Scottish boarder and all the soda bread Kitty baked every Friday to sell to the local grocer, John Monteverdi, barely met their weekly obligations. More often than not, John Dodd's meager paycheck experienced a regular transfer from legal tender to liquored libations. The transactions took place in bars attached to factories along Bloomfield Avenue, from the Oranges to Newark, and back.

When Jim Ryan had married Kitty's other daughter, Lillian, some financial stability came to the household along with Jim's promise to Kitty that he'd never let alcohol into the family's rented home. Often he tracked his father-in-law's liquor-fueled wanderings to bring him safely back to Liberty Street. But then Jim enlisted in the Coast Guard to do his part for the war effort, and was sent to Atlantic City. And so came the night when John Dodd never made it back to Kitty's bed.

That was forty-eight hours ago. As a search party fanned out along the boundary of Eagle Rock, a worker at the amusement park, where the family had spent happier times, found John's body floating in Crystal Lake.

John had loved Mariah's high-spirited nature, and was proud of her nursing degree. Her salary helped put food on the table. But in private, John continued to drink to distance her achievements with his dwindling ability to provide enough for his other children and Kitty. Not even his sons' pending arrival from Brest, France was enough to get John to relent on what had become nightly benders.

Her two youngest children, Kitty's boys had enlisted in the Navy. Their first paying job was helping to convert the *USS George Washington* from an ocean liner to a troop transport ship at the Brooklyn naval yard. Then, three months after Mariah's death and shortly before the Christmas of 1917, they left for Europe. Kitty thanked the Holy Father the pair had never seen combat. Instead, the brothers parlayed their naval-yard steam-fitting skills into on-board ship maintenance; both were worthy trades that would make it easier for them to get factory work when the war was over and America resumed its peace-time economy.

Even more thrilling was the brothers' opportunity to meet President Woodrow Wilson, New Jersey's former governor. The president promised to find "his Jersey lads" jobs with Thomas Edison, no less. But instead of a celebration that heralded this positive turn in the family's fortunes, the boys' homecoming was marked by a funeral mass for their father at St. John's. Even Jim merited early release from his maritime surveillance to make it up from Atlantic City to the Oranges in time for John Dodd's wake.

Like her mother, Lillian lay awake. She, too, was alone in her married bed. It was socially unacceptable to make the rounds of various saloons where her husband and brothers were waking her father. Unlike her mother's worries about the family's finances, Lil, was mad and chose to curse the Angel of Death, and all the saints she could remember were associated with liquor: St. George, St. Adrian, St. Arnold, St. Leger, and St. Martin. For good measure, Lil cursed St. Valentine, too.

At the end of her silent tirade she stopped to remember just why it was she had fallen in love with that big lug of an Irishman from New York City. Was it his open face, free of any obvious guile? That thick wavy, coal-black hair so different from her round-faced, straight-haired brothers? Was it the way he held her on the dance floor where she had passed for being older than 17 to gain entrance to the Fenian Fund Dance at the Irish Patrolmen's Club in Newark?

More debonair than all the boys she'd met in the Oranges, Jim Ryan was older. He was more street-smart than the local crowd, and more calmly self-assured. His confidence told everyone he didn't have to prove himself. Jim could hold his liquor, too, and always knew when to stop.

Or, did her heart find room it didn't know she had because of the tender care he bestowed on his infant daughter even as he continued to care for his wayward father-in-law? The Shepherd, that's what her mother nicknamed him, after Lil brought him home for the family's approval. They had taken to him, alright, and Jim was out with the men of the family right now. Lil then cursed her husband for leaving her alone and cursed the fact that women, except for those who could only find a livelihood in saloons, were still barred from drinking in public.

When she had two-stepped with him at the annual Fenian, Lil told Jim she wanted a man to sweep her off her feet and take her far away from the humdrum world she saw in the Oranges. He could take her to his people in cosmopolitan Manhattan, if he so desired. But pulling her closer to him, Jim murmured in Lil's ear that circumstances weren't right for his return to New York. That he wanted to make a new life for himself on this side of the Hudson River. That there was work for him in Jersey that drew on his analytical skills with numbers, though he'd have to be away from home for long stretches of time when the weather was good. His musky warmth. His protective strength. Lil deferred her big-city dream and let Jim Ryan marry her. John Dodd said little and Kitty willingly accommodated her only son-in-law, grateful that all his worldly possessions came with him in one small cardboard suitcase. Baby Doris arrived soon thereafter. Times were tough, and Lil had to go back to work at U.S. Radium where she painted luminescent numbers on clocks of all sizes.

"I don't want my granddaughter glowing in the dark," Kitty stated flatly in a debate that erupted after Doris was born. Kitty distrusted the way in which her daughter had to lick the tip of the paint brush to create a fine point with which to draw the phosphate lines. But money was in short supply, and Lil's paycheck, less than the hourly wage for men who worked assembly at the radium company, was sorely needed.

On some sacred list of saints names, there's got to be one for radium, Lil reasoned. For good measure, she decided to curse him too.

"Jesus, Mary, and Saint Joseph!"

Doris hesitated, her right hand on the knob to her parents' bedroom door.

"What are you doing up at this hour?" Lillian asked, her voice assuming a slightly more gentle tone. "Daddy will be home soon. So will your Uncle Pete and Uncle Frank.

"And if President Wilson caves in and says yes to all the noise about banning the 'demon rum', maybe all the bars will dry up and the men in this household will, too! Though it won't have happened in time to save your granddad."

Lillian felt a lump rise in her throat.

"Now, go on. Go back to bed before your father comes home."

Doris quietly closed the door. But instead of walking back down the hall to the boarder's old bedroom that was now hers, she moved to the front of the house. At her grandmother's door she stood a moment, then rapped softly.

"Come in, child." Kitty had expected Doris after hearing Lillian's loud, startled oath. Truth was, Kitty loved her granddaughter, even more these last two years as the Dodd resemblance in Mariah started to blossom. Lillian and her brothers were Scottish Irish: redheaded, blue-eyed, freckled, loud, and occasionally stubborn. A little like Kitty whose own red hair was turning to pale auburn as she got older. Mariah had been more like John: Celtic dark with blue eyes that seemed to go from a pale gray to cornflower blue, depending on her mood. Doris was noticeably more reserved, almost shy by comparison. Kitty observed the quieter, solemn temperament in her eight-year-old granddaughter, and saw in it a chance to dream again about the freedom she had come to America to find.

"Here. You can lie next to me." Kitty moved to occupy John's side of the double bed, and Doris climbed up to lay next to her grandmother.

"Your wee life is only going to get better," said Kitty. "You'll see. You're going to continue with your education after you get out of high school. You're going to get a good, decent job that's not in a factory."

She paused to tuck a lock of hair behind Doris's right ear.

"President Wilson is supporting a law that's going to give me, your mother, and, one day when you're old enough, even you the right to vote. That's something I didn't even have in Ireland. One day you're going to become a young lady with more possibilities than either one of us may ever have in our entire lifetime.

Kitty gave a sigh that was part defiance, part contentment. "You'll see. We women really do run everything," she continued, "but we'll finally have the legal stockings to stand in and make change happen. This, my child, I promise you."

Faintly, from a distance, Kitty could hear the sounds of all three men returning home.

"Here, now, I'll walk you back to your room and help you into bed. Your father will be home before you know it, and soon it will be time for breakfast. Come on."

The July heat, trapped by day in Pleasant Valley, had evaporated in the moonlight, replaced with cool night air. But as the moon slowly slipped away behind the Watchung Range, the sun's first faint rays of the morning were rising east over Newark Bay, straining to reach the perimeter of the valley and illuminate the boys' long walk home. The last trolley had stopped running hours ago and the trio wasn't in a hurry to make its way back from the Horn Place Chop House, the final bar down at Main and Essex Streets where they had waked John Dodd and feted their own return from the war to end all wars.

Hard to believe that just a few short days ago they had been aboard the *USS George Washington* with Woodrow Wilson, steaming back one last time to the United States from Europe. On June 28, President Wilson signed the Treaty of Versailles. Then on July 4, he and King Albert of Belgium, and their wives, spent the entire day on deck where sailors from both countries put on a series of spectaculars to entertain the jubilant heads of state. One was an exhibition boxing match. Pete had fought the fight of his career!

"Com' on," said Pete, putting up his fists to his brother Frank whose whistling had turned to song. "One more time."

In the middle of Liberty Street Pete started to lean on the balls of his rather large feet.

"Mademoiselle from Armentièere par ley voo,," Frank kept singing,

even as he cocked his elbows.

"The mademoiselle from Armentièere she hasn't been kissed for forty years," he warbled, *"Hinky, dinky par ley voo."*

Then he feinted a right swing and pulled up his left fist, just as he had always done in every practice session on board ship that he'd put his older brother through.

Pete stepped back and thrust two quick jabs – right-left, right-left – at Frank.

Frank danced backwards, mimicking the prance of his brother's Belgian contender. A bantam weight, Frank had been a boxer in his own right, with his moment of glory before the war. His brother, Pete, was a welter weight, and so was the Belgian navy man he sparred with on deck. They had gone three rounds before Pete landed a stunning knock-out punch that sent his opponent toes-up.

"One, two, three..." Jim Ryan stepped in as the referee, as thoroughly versed in this particular war story as he was in the brothers' boyhood dream of becoming professional boxers. Then, quickly changing roles, he became President Wilson.

"Why, I see you two boys look like. Are you related?"

"Yessir!" Pete piped up. "We're the Fighting Dodds from the Oranges. This here's my brother, Frankie, who had the title fight two years ago in Laurel Gardens in Newark."

"And this is my older brother, Peter." Frank affected a deep, serious tone. "Among fellow pugilists he's known to train to the sounds of: Ray, Ray, Ray, Tiger, Tiger, Tiger."

The three men start laughing uproariously at the Princeton fight song and Wilson's one-time connection as university president to the orange-and-black mascot.

"Dead on, Frankie," Pete commented. "All those bits of songs you pick up came in handy."

Jim continued his role as President Wilson.

"Did you vote for me?"

"Oh, yes. Our mum and sister would have voted for you too, several times, if they had the right."

Jim paused. President Wilson took seriously the political pitch for women's suffrage.

"I guess you haven't heard. Congress agreed to the 19th Amendment last month. We've got to get a majority of the states to ratify it now. I endorsed this proposal. I'm married to a woman, after all."

Jim Ryan broke character and chortled.

"My life as a married man will be over."

Then he cleared his throat.

"Well, what you going to do after the Navy?" he asked, resuming his role as Wilson.

"We hope to work for Thomas Edison," Pete answered.

A little cloud of concern passed over the president's face.

"Thomas Edison, one of the greatest men of our time." Again, he paused. "He and I are having a little dispute on labor matters at the moment.

"When you have a dispute with Edison," he continued slowly, "you also have a dispute with Ford and Firestone."

Mindful of the press pool which had traveled with him on every trip across the Atlantic, Wilson then suspended his conversation. It had reported every maneuver of his diplomatic footwork in Paris as he sparred with Georges Clemenceau over the Allies' Fourteen Points.

"Well, Mr. President," Pete quipped, "I guess we shouldn't use you as a reference."

At this Jim as President Wilson burst out laughing, drawing the attention of the idling imaginary photographers.

"Well, he did vote for me," he said. "I'll put in a good word for you boys."

Now assuming the role of a photographer, Jim swarmed around the brothers even as he kept them walking homeward.

"Let's line you boys up with the president. The folks back home will enjoy seeing you in the all the papers."

There was little need to re-enact the homecoming at the pier in Hoboken when the *Washington* docked. There, amid the waving Stars and Stripes and American Red Cross flags, Kitty, Lillian and Doris stood, hand-in-hand, the smile on their faces trying to hide the obvious: John, the Dodd family patriarch, was not on hand to greet them.

Kitty returned to her bedroom just as she heard the men climbing the steps to the front stoop. She'd give them this one extra day off. They'd be too hung over to make a favorable impression during a job interview with Thomas Edison, regardless of President Wilson's recommendation. The inventor had gone on public record against alcohol, and she didn't want her sons to ruin their chances of getting a factory job by showing up in less than perfect fitness.

The family needed their steady paychecks. Kitty was still determined that Lillian quit her job at that infernal radium plant. None of the boys' military paychecks had helped them much during the two years they were gone. Now that all three were home again, steady money from steady work was needed to keep food on the table and their heads above water. And, so that Doris would have a better future than any of them, Kitty vowed.

If she couldn't achieve the American dream, by God and all that is holy in the name of St. Anne Shandon of Cork, her granddaughter would. She turned from the window to return to her empty bed.

Had Kitty lingered she might have glimpsed the tall, spare figure who hung back at the top of the street where Liberty met Main, watching as Pete, Frank, and Jim walked the final yards to the Dodd house.

Jock Sanders rubbed his right hand over the scared knuckles of his left. One day the boys would slip up and he'd get them. One day. But not in an obvious way. Not after burying their old man. No. He wanted to settle the score over what had happened to him in Sam McGee's gym long before the war had begun. And get revenge for Lil's laughing rejection of his affections, choosing that New York racketeer over him. While the brothers were away, Sanders had bulked up at a KKK training camp in Tillman Ravine. Landing a job on the Oranges Police Department couldn't have happened at a better time.

Chapter 2: After the Famine, 1869

Colm Kelleher called his eldest daughter over to the window. "Kitty, come look see."

Colm gestured through the partially opened curtain. Kitty heard the disciplined footsteps of men, marching in synchronized rhythm. As the five-year-old reached the window to stand next to her father, a small formation of British military soldiers dressed in black and tan passed by.

"They're getting exercise before they board ship in the harbor," Colm explained. "There's probably going to be a war in India, and we'll be rid of them...for a while anyway. If you come upon them in the road, always look straight ahead. Don't look over your shoulder. Don't frown. Don't smile. Don't engage."

Colm stopped, and twisted his fingers across his lips as though he were buttoning a coat.

"Always be aware that even out of uniform, the damn Brits are somewhere," he added. "They own our land. They take our herds.

They tax us to death. But one day, *one day*, there'll be a reckoning, right Bridie?"

Colm turned to his heavily pregnant wife, the once girlish Bridget Power, tending to his three younger daughters still in nappies.

"We'll have us a son next, won't we," he said, not so much asking, but stating a fervent hope as fact. "A Fenian who'll make us proud and free."

"Don't go believing everything you read in *The Irish People*," Bridie said, gently admonishing her husband's yearning for liberation. The pro-independence newspaper alternated between supporting Prime Minister William Gladstone's efforts at granting them rule and threatening violence if London's Parliament didn't give the Irish their independence. "You take to blowing up ships in Cork Harbor or sabotaging the supply wagons the family builds, and the first place they'll come looking at is the Power-Kelleher farm."

Bridie's family had been wagoneers for over two hundred years. They had survived the on-going British occupation, just barely. Good with creating a steady, even temperature at the family forge, Colm's skill kept the Power boys working at shoeing horses and making the iron rigging for wagons. Just like nearly all the Irish, they had to pay rent to the British for their land. But the two families evened out their perpetual deficit with a contract from the Royal Naval Command on Haulbowline Island in Cork Harbor. They built and maintained the wagons that brought grain and beef supplies from the outlaying countryside to the military ships.

"We're not the problem, we're the solution," Colm retorted. "At least the next generation is. Whether they're boys or girls, I supposed," he broke off to look again at Kitty, "we're raising the new band of Fenian warriors to avenge the loss of our fathers who died in ditches when the Great Famine fell upon us. We're entitled to a divorce from Britain."

Kitty listened solemnly to her father. Even at her young age, she was familiar with his stock political rantings. She and her cousins knew they were the hope of the older generation's desire for independence and, perhaps, a little vengeance.

"Here, child," he said, "go get ready to help me make these deliveries."

Colm moved over to the hearth in the family's long, one-room stone cottage. A peat-burning fireplace anchored the wall where the babies slept and Bridie rocked in a chair, crocheting a new receiving blanket.

"*Do-o-na. No-o-bis,*" Colm crooned as reverentially as though he were in church reciting Latin prayers. "*Po-tche-en, po-tcheen.*"

Small clay jugs filled with *poitín* cooled on the hearth, a dozen pints in all. Getting her mother's egg basket, Kitty knew they wouldn't return before dark. She and her Da would make their deliveries on foot, house to house, because using the horses would draw too much attention. Her father always came away from each croft with money in his pocket, a magical exchange for the alcohol distilled from the blend of potato mash, yeast, and sugar that all afternoon boiled merrily in a large stock pot over the fire. It was a sideline Colm had developed with his understanding of temperature and timing. His customers were people, like him, who did not want to pay the British tax on merchandise.

"Let's go, Kitty, and play hide-and-seek-in-plain-sight."

Kitty switched trolleys by the bronze statue of Father Matthew, Cork's leading temperance crusader. She sometimes believed the priest had colluded with the British as part of a covert effort to put farmers like her father out of the home-brewing business. Colm had moved beyond *poitin,* and now was making sour mash whiskey from recycled fermented grains of rye. He still did his sideline in stealth, only he used Kitty's younger sisters as his helpers. As Kitty reached her teenage years, her parents had decided their eldest would purse her comprehensives; Colm because he wanted Kitty to be closer to the port's activities, Bridie because she wanted her first-born to break away from marrying a farmer and making babies. Colm had sired eight daughters and no sons, and still he wanted to try again. Truth be told, Bridie was getting tired. The family needed the income of another adult if there were any more babies. Kitty was maturing into a young lady with a good head for figures and a fine penmanship. Though she had learned the domestic art of baking bread and crocheting, it was clear her younger sisters could more readily help with the traditional chores so Kitty could make the daily trek into Cork proper and pursue a formal education. Besides, the pool of eligible bachelors seemed to shrink with every girl Colm Kelleher sired, and Bridie didn't want her girls to marry a local boy out of desperation.

Earlier in the morning, Colm had pulled Kitty aside and told her the British needed someone who could write in legible cursive at their command office on Haulbowline. He explained where to go and how to apply for the position. So instead of going directly to school, Kitty found herself switching from the second trolley to a small ferry that took her across the River Lee. The Union Jack was prominently flying over the rooftops of Queenstown, the name the damn Brits, as Kitty cursed them, had substituted for her native Cork.

Get the job, Kitty, her father had insisted; we've got to infiltrate their ranks. They'll never suspect the fairer sex. Kitty kept her contempt in check as she disembarked from the ferry. The Union Jack was flying from a tower, beneath which a sign informed her that this was command headquarters. Kitty took a deep breath, and as she exhaled, she opened the door.

"Can I help you, miss?"

The naval officer sitting behind the desk appraised the slender teenager, her auburn hair pulled back in a tidy braided bun, blue eyes snapping as they adjusted from the cold to the meager warmth thrown off by the room's small fireplace. Behind him a long table with a vacant chair occupied the wall beneath a window. Stacks of papers in discrete piles lined its entire length. To the right of the table was a door leading deeper into the stone fortification. A naval guard stood at attention, his rifle positioned across the front of his uniform.

"I've come for the job…" Kitty hesitated, then started again with a little more force. "I'm applying for the clerk's post. I was told you need help with forms."

Officer Oliver Jones hadn't expected much cooperation from the locals, but he knew times were tough so he shouldn't have been surprised if a female came in for the job. He gave a curt nod and motioned Kitty over to the table behind him. "Sit here." He turned back to his desk and opened a drawer, pulling out a sheaf of blank paper. From another drawer he pulled a bottle of ink and a quill. "Here."

Kitty took the implements and placed them on the table. Unhooking the top two buttons of her black cloak, but leaving it on to keep her warm, she sat down in the chair.

Officer Jones leaned over and handed her a bill of lading he had been examining. "Copy this. All of it. To this blank page." His directive came out in short bursts.

Kitty looked at the unlined paper. She then lined up its bottom edge with that of the table, took the stopper out of the bottle, dipped the finely honed quill, and started writing at the top of the page. Thirty minutes later the entire form, both the typed column headers and all the hand-written information had been transposed, letter for letter, line by line, onto the previously empty piece of paper. Kitty took a deep breath and slowly let it out.

"It's finished."

The officer scraped his chair back, got up and turned to lean over Kitty. He gave a quick start of surprise at the evenly spaced lines of handwritten figures, content, destinations, and timetables, then quickly recovered himself.

"All those pages have to be copied," he said with a sweep of his hand across the piles, "when dried, they have to filed."

Kitty gasped.

"If you want this job, it will handily take you three weeks. That's a backlog, and there's more coming in because of trouble in the Suez."

Officer Jones stopped. His eyes drilled into her.

"Or, you can leave now."

Kitty found a reservoir of calm as she recalled one of her father's admonishments: don't frown, don't smile. Kitty returned his look.

"I will do this work for you," she began in an even tone, carefully enunciating each word, dry of any emotion. "But I would like to continue with my comprehensives. I will give you measure for measure. Might I come here in the afternoons? I will work weekends, if I have to."

Office Jones blinked. He hadn't anticipated any negotiation. Most of the Irish took without question the menial garrison jobs. Granted, this was a cut above menial even though, he smiled inwardly, it was hand labor.

"Every afternoon at twelve sharp."

Kitty nodded. She'd arrange with her instructors to turn in her class work early. As the morning was nearly gone, Kitty turned back to the table and began copying the next bill.

"The Suez, eh?" Colm quizzed Kitty out by the forge where he was cleaning up for the day. Her cousins, boys every one of them from Powers to Oats to Finnegans, gathered around to listen to what Kitty had gleaned from her afternoon at the command post.

"You get a look at any correspondence?"

"Something came in today from Portsmouth."

Colm nodded in recognition of where the Royal Navy built its new ships.

"You're going to need to find a way to see the signatures," he told Kitty. Then turning to his nephews, he announced: "Boys, we're going to form us a phantom Fenian battalion!"

As the weeks of winter rolled into spring, Colm's plan to feed the families and stockpile munitions took root and Kitty found high-level signatures and set about imitating them until her father couldn't tell the difference between what was hers and what was signed by various commanding officers on the island and in England.

"The next mail that comes in from Portsmouth, you're going to swap in a letter directing Officer Jones to reroute supplies off the ships and to the battalion," Colm told Kitty.

"We'll get the Oat and Finnegan boys to take the dray horses and wagons in to fetch the supplies," he continued. "They've never been into Cork, so they won't be recognized."

The logistics were a lot more difficult than Colm had realized. First a letter to the high command had to be written to redirect a supply ship bound to Gibraltar to Cork instead. Then a second letter, to Officer Jones, had to be written, directing the supplies be removed from the ship, placed on wagons requisitioned from the home office, and delivered to a secure but secret outpost deep in the Nagle Mountains. The letter would indicate the drivers had been thoroughly vetted by Portsmouth officials.

Instead of the battalion of one thousand men that Colm had

envisioned, Kitty rewrote the second directive to explain that at the highest level of cooperation between the Royal Army and Royal Navy, an elite platoon of forty-four men were training for maneuvers in preparation for deployment to the Suez. Kitty reasoned that supplies for one thousand Brits mustering up in Ireland might rouse suspicion. A platoon, on the other hand, seemed more probable, especially until Colm's master plan of stockpiling enough food, clothing, and munitions was complete. The order made clear that no questions were anticipated from Officer Jones or any of his men at Haulbowline and that the directive was to be placed in a safe and never consulted.

The military floats on a sea of paper they don't read, Kitty thought to herself. This plan should work.

While copying the latest batch of invoices and waiting for the afternoon mail to come, Kitty noticed Officer Jones was in a chatty mood, though his conversation was directed to the young guard in charge of the garrison door.

"So, Harry, did you hear that just before getting out of Kilmainham Gaol Charles Parnell swore allegiance to the Irish Republican Brotherhood?

"And, he's not been out three days and already he's been spotted in Dublin with Captain O'Shea's wife, Kitty. How long do you think the Irish Catholics are going to back an Anglo pol that cuckolds one of their captains?"

Officer Jones looked over at Kitty.

"Home rule gets farther away once you let women get involved in politics."

Kitty could feel Officer Jones' eyes on her back, but she kept up with the transfers she was copying. Hidden in the never-ending piles of paper was the requisition for rerouting the supply ships and the directive for telling Officer Jones to follow HQ's orders without question. Kitty sent up a silent prayer to Saint Finbarr of Cork that today opportunity would present itself so she could mail the naval envelopes where they needed to go.

Just then Officer Jones indicated to Harry his need to get inside the garrison. "Got to get me to the loo. Must be something I ate this morning for breakfast."

Harry stepped aside the door and let him pass into the fort. Then, just as nimbly, he stepped back in front of the door. Kitty kept up with her copying, steady, slow, measured, never once pausing. Harry had no sooner repositioned his rifle than the outside door opened and the petty officer came in with the afternoon mail bag.

"This one's a heavy one today," he announced. "What do you have going out?"

Kitty let a moment lapse before she put her pen down. "Let me get you the outbound mail." She picked up a stack of envelopes, then turned back around to Officer Jones' desk where the mail bag lay on the floor, filled with most of her work from earlier that afternoon.

"Here's the last of them," she said, cinching the pouch and handing it across the desk.

"Thank you, ma'am." The petty office officer touched his fingers to the top of his cap and winked at Kitty.

Later that spring evening, after getting off the island ferry, Kitty lingered along the quay before catching the trolley. It was Friday, after all, and while she was not yet of age to go to a pub, Kitty did yearn to stay out late and experience some of the night life Cork might offer, even if it only meant looking through well-lit windows to see how families better off than hers lived.

She continued to stroll across the stone bulkhead where thousands of her countrymen had gathered to leave for America in the wake of the potato famine. Kitty allowed herself a rare moment of reverie: I wonder what America is like? A democratic country that no longer belonged to the empire-building British; a place where foreigners could start their lives fresh, leaving behind old politics and grudge matches; where men and women could have an honest grub stake in building a new country.

A fine mist began to fall. Kitty noticed further down the quay that on a separate pier a large ferry had berthed and was disgorging passengers. Ahead of everyone else, a stranger approached in her direction. He walked with purpose, she noticed. As she drew closer, Kitty also observed the ferry was one that regularly shuttled between Cork and Liverpool. Time to get the first of her two trolleys and go home, she thought; she didn't want to mix with any Englishmen. Just as Kitty started to turn, the stranger's voice called out to her.

"Excuse me, miss. Can you tell me the best way to get to Tiknock?"

Kitty momentarily froze. Tiknock was the pretty little crossroads village the supply wagons had to pass through on the way to the phantom training camp in the Nagle Mountains. No, no, the directive couldn't have been intercepted on this ferry. But was there something she needed to know from this Englishman about the tiny village? Kitty turned back.

"It's too late to get a livery to take you there," she said.

"My gran is expecting me no matter what the hour or if I have to walk." A Gaelic lilt tinged his pronunciation of the word gran.

"Really, now, and I suppose you're going to tell me you're Honora Burke's grandson!" Kitty taunted him to see what he knew of Irish history.

A broad grin spread across the young man's face, and Kitty saw for the first time that a narrow well-trimmed coal-black mustache adorned his upper lip. A bachelor, she noted.

"Well, Nano Burke would have had to plead Immaculate Conception, so busy was she starting the Order of the Presentation Nuns to have birthed a family. Don't tell me, you're one of their graduates?"

Kitty blushed. The stranger had done her one better.

"Permit me to introduce myself," he continued. "My name is John Dodd. Before you go thinking of me as one of those dirty Protestants, let me assure you that my gran was born a Healy here in County Cork. But my father's father died in England after I was born, and Gran decided to come back to Tiknock," he broke off to take a breath, "and truth be told she didn't get along with my mum.

"Gran came back and married a Gilhooly to set it right with Healys. None of this marrying for love the second time around," he added, a soft sing-song rhythm beginning to lace his extended speech. "Now that I'm of age, I'm free to visit her whenever I want. This is my first journey since getting a job in the harbor office in Liverpool. I had to save up six months' pay to buy the ticket, so I don't have enough money for a livery."

Kitty was vaguely aware that somewhere on her father's side of the blanket there was a Power who had married a Healy. She also noticed her attraction to this stranger. Though her father had raised her to distrust anyone he hadn't introduced to her, Kitty thought her mother might approve of this man dressed in a suit who had a job in a harbor office. Turning again towards the trolley station, Kitty motioned for John to follow along beside her.

"My name is Kitty Kelleher and I'm taking the trolley home. Maybe my da can help you get to Tiknock."

An hour and a half later, Kitty and John arrived at the Kelleher's low-lying cottage on the outskirts of Cork. Kitty opened the front door, announcing she'd brought home a guest. Her youngest sisters tumbled out of their bunks while the older ones turned from tending dinner that bubbled in the large iron pot in the hearth. Bridie looked up from her rocking chair to appraise the man who had stepped from behind her daughter. She imperceptibly nodded to Kitty.

Just then Colm stomped behind her on the flagstone the family used for a front step.

"Here, you're home." Colm's voice boomed deliberately so the stranger in the city clothes would hear him.

Kitty turned to make the introductions. The two men shook hands and Colm invited John to a chair from the family's only table. "What's your business in these parts?"

Realizing he was being evaluated, John spooled out all the stories he knew about his grandfather's family in rural Cork. Widowed for a second time, Gran was getting on in years and he wanted to pay his respects while she still remembered him. John admitted he had underestimated what it would take to travel from Cork to Tiknock after an all-day journey on the ferry. He had earned but four days off for this entire sojourn. Might Kitty's family oblige him in some small way?

Colm led the young man to the barn where he saddled a draught mare. Then, pointing to the north road, Colm told John the ride would take him at most two hours. Wishing him well, he slapped the old mare on the rump, and horse and rider disappeared into the darkness.

"Well, my dear, we'll see just what kind of man you brought home come the morrow."

John Dodd did return in the morning, leading the mare behind a black-and-white cob horse. Colm was impressed with the handsome work horse John rode, but his envy was fleeting. John leaned down from the cob and as he handed over the mare's reins he shared with

Colm the political news he picked up in Tiknock. Parliament had recently appointed Frederick Cavenish chief secretary for Ireland. The country's permanent under secretary was Thomas Burke.

"Cavenish and Burke were stabbed to death yesterday in Phoenix Park," John said.

"Word is the Fenians are behind this. If you have any plans, lay low because the Brits and Parnell's people, both, will be looking at anyone urging violence to claim home rule at this time."

Startled by John's grasp of politics despite his age and English last name, Colm blinked his eyes several times to indicate he understood.

"That said, there's more trouble for Parliament abroad," John added. "The Brits don't have enough reserves to reinforce the regular army so they're going to ship veteran soldiers down to the Suez. They're stretched pretty thin, so there might be other opportunities to exploit that aren't so obvious."

Before reeling his horse around for the return trip to Tiknock, John looked more intensely at Colm.

"I look forward to the opportunity to court your daughter, Kitty." With those final words, John departed up the hard-packed dirt road.

The weeks and months that followed were filled with contentious political events as the Battle of Tel el Kebir broke out in Egypt and the House of Lords debated the merits of invading Burma in order to expand the British Empire beyond India. Against this background of international affairs, military supplies intended for the Suez found their way, instead, to the Nagle Mountains hideaway. Colm's plan of rerouting the provisions worked! The Power-Kelleher Clan stockpiled enough provisions to last them through the following winter. In time Kitty forged a new directive to send food and equipment to the garrison command on Gibraltar, thereby deflating interest by her superiors who had begun to discuss the possibility of meeting the elite corps training northwest of Tiknock.

But even as the families' daily life seemed to improve, Colm's vision for an Ireland free of British domination dimmed when the House of Lords voted down the much hoped-for home rule bill that would have granted the Irish more of a say in how they were governed.

Throughout everything, a correspondence between Kitty and John blossomed. Kitty shared dreams of finishing school and finding a teaching job so she wouldn't have to work for the British Navy anymore. And if that didn't happened, she wondered what it might be like to board one of the ships in Cork Harbor and go to America. Twice a year, John managed to visit his grandmother, setting time aside to spend with Kitty and her family. One day he wanted to marry and start a family, he wrote her. As a show of his intentions, John told Kitty he was saving all his pub money. Could she wait until he had set aside enough for the both of them?

Kitty agreed to wait. Then, as a new home-rule bill wound its way through the House of Lords and the Irish allowed their hopes to rise again with expectation, John asked Colm for Kitty's hand in marriage, agreeing to send the Kelleher family money until the first grandchild arrived.

But when the British Lords refused to grant Ireland's new petition for self governance, John Dodd made a fateful decision. Kitty told her husband she was pregnant and John decided their first-born's future was destined to unfold in another country. Money intended as his last marriage payment to Colm Kelleher instead went to buy immediate passage for him, his wife, and their unborn child on a ship bound for New York.

Kitty wanted a fresh start for her new family, too, but leaving without even telling her mother farewell tore a hole in her heart.

The couple stood on the aft deck, watching Cork become smaller as their ship pulled away from the quay. In one hand Kitty clutched a small ink sketch of Cork Harbor John had impetuously bought so she would always have a piece of Ireland with her. Suddenly, bursts of light flashed and the thundering sound of explosions occurred. Kitty protectively put her other hand on her belly and smiled ruefully. Perhaps her father had known she was leaving after all. A few years back he had taught her how to make dynamite look like coal. A couple of days ago, the Oats and Finnegans had delivered a load of coal to the British ships docked in port. All it took was time before the heat in the boilers exploded with the fake fuel's hidden gunpowder.

Two weeks later, Kitty and John again stood on the ship's deck, this time their eyes riveted to the Statue of Liberty that loomed ever large as the ship made its way into New York Harbor. It was good to get out of steerage and into the fresh air. Even better it was to look at their new country, a panoramic skyline filled with tall buildings and piers up the Hudson River as far as their eyes could see.

In Manhattan, the Dodds joined other third-class passengers who were herded onto a barge and transported to Ellis Island, the new immigration center that had opened the previous year in 1892. The couple spent three hours on a line for the required medical inspection. Despite her very obvious pregnancy, Kitty was not deemed a health risk and was cleared to proceed. There followed two more hours on line to take the legal exam to determine their suitability for citizenship. John did most of the talking, using his English accent to speak for the both of them. Near the end, as Kitty started visibly to tire, Immigration Inspector Paul Mulgrew showed a moment of softness towards the young couple and inquired if they knew how to find their family.

John gave a start.

"I live in Newark, on the Orange side," Mulgrew explained. "Everyone knows the Dodds. They've been there since the Revolution."

Mulgrew smiled, and gave the final stamp to their papers. "Take the Jersey City ferry, then look for the Orange trolley line. It will take you clear through Newark and out to the Oranges. Best of luck to you."

Flour, baking soda, buttermilk, salt: Kitty put the ingredients for making her weekly delivery of soda bread to John Monteverdi on the table beside last night's edition of the *Newark Evening News*, January 16, 1920. Her son-in-law Jim Ryan stood at the kitchen sink, paring his finger nails with a pen knife. A suitcase was located at the doorway to the dining room.

"Our President Wilson was against it," Kitty began. "He's no fool. Enforcing the Anti-Saloon League's amendment to the Constitution will be impossible!"

Her finger underlining the words in the newspaper, Kitty read out loud, " 'No one can make alcohol, sell it, barter for it, import or export it, nor transport it.'

"What's going to happen to Tom McNichols at Rheingold? Where's he going to get another job driving a truck? What's going to happen to those bars where you conduct your business?" Kitty inhaled deeply.

"It's been five months since John died and old man Edison doesn't pay the boys as much as he does his muckers."

Turning away from the newspaper, she added, "You know Lil should stop working at that damn radium factory."

Jim sighed patiently, putting away his pen knife.

"Well, at least Mrs. Tierney will be sleeping better knowing all her Women's Christian Temperance Union work paid off."

"Jim, don't go changing the subject," Kitty said. "Each one of us here on Liberty Street is going to be affected if the bars are closed."

"If I were a betting man," Jim responded, half in jest, "I'd say the first document Governor-elect Edwards puts his name to after he's sworn into office is his veto against the Federal Prohibition Amendment.

"Let me see what I can find out down in Florida," he added. "There are new horses the stables are running at Hialeah to see how they might race at Saratoga and Belmont this summer. I'll ask around to see if the smart money thinks liquor will ever be outlawed nationwide."

Peeling off several bills from his wallet, and handing them to Kitty, Jim added, "Oh, look, here comes your favorite boy, Jimmy Jimmy."

In the same moment that she heard the clip-clop of horses' hooves, Kitty looked through her kitchen window to see the vegetable wagon pull up in front of their house. Kitty walked Jim down the front steps and to the sidewalk where he pecked his mother-in-law on the cheek, waved and walked up Liberty Street.

"Mrs. D.! How nice to see you this crisp winter morning. Here, let me give you my lap blanket to keep you warm."

Jimmy Jimmy carefully arranged the tattered wool cloth around Kitty's shoulders, letting one arm linger as an anchor should the cover slip away. Kitty smiled.

"Well, Jimmy, what did you bring this week?"

"Good news for me, Mrs. D.! This is the last of the deliveries I'll be making. I'm retiring Old Ted, here, and buying me a delivery truck!"

"Why, Jimmy, business must be booming."

"Naw…I've been saving my money. With my son and nephew coming of age, I'm looking to change my business and go wholesale so they'll have jobs," he slowed. "I can't compete with the likes of John Monteverdi and the neighborhood grocery stores like his all over the Oranges. But, I can supply him! We've already made a deal."

Kitty gave a sad little smile. Jimmy Jimmy was a widower, several years her junior, and she knew he had a soft spot for her. But one husband had been enough, and so long as the family's finances were still in trouble, Kitty felt that she needed to keep the Dodd family together, not create a bigger family.

"I'll miss you, Jimmy," she said. "Why don't you make it a point to come to this year's Paddy-Purim Parade? All the housewives will love to have you sit with them as their husbands and children take part in Liberty Street's annual rite of spring."

Jimmy nodded, acknowledging the invitation. "I'd like that, especially if I could sit next to you Mrs. D."

On cue, Kitty blushed.

"What vegetables to you have today?"

They went around to the rear of the wagon and as Kitty made her selection of winter vegetables, she asked Jimmy Jimmy for a second bag of potatoes, a second pound of sugar, and a cake of yeast. He raised his eyebrows, but thought better of asking any questions.

"Why don't we make this last order on me, and I'll carry all of it in the house for you myself?"

Kitty began to protest.

"No, Mrs. D., all I want in payment is an extra loaf of that wonderful bread you bake to sell at Montevederi's, whether it's your traditional recipe from Ireland," he said, "or a new potato bread you're trying out."

Kitty reflected a moment at the cover story Jimmy Jimmy had given her.

"Okay, then, come back around later and you'll see what I've made."

"Kitty, you ready to join us here at the curb?"

Despite her years of living in the Oranges, Peggy McNichols, who hailed from Ballynoe, couldn't soften the brogue in her spoken English. A gregarious, fun-loving individual, Peggy had been delighted to introduce Kitty to the neighborhood. It was Peggy who first heard the news that Ireland had turned the religious holiday devoted to St. Patrick into a grand one for all the public to enjoy. Kitty and Peggy seized on the turn of events to have their young children put together a parade with second-hand instruments the two women had begged and borrowed from their extensive network of friends at St. John's parish.

Peggy motioned to the space between her and Helen Smith, Liberty Street's newest housewife.

The Smiths had just moved in over the winter, having sold their Glen Ridge house to pay a lawyer in Mr. Smith's patent fight with Thomas Edison. The irony wasn't wasted on the Smiths. Not only had they wound up in a rental house within the shadows of Edison's extensive factories, but their son, Mike, a decorated World War I soldier ~ a Bronze Star pinned by General John Pershing for Mike's valor as a tank driver at the Battle of Saint Mihiel, right beside Captain George Patten, no less ~ had to take a job working in Edison's paint shop. This was Mike's day off, and he and his still-precocious sister, Pat, were finding their place in the Paddy-Purim line-up. Mike carried a battered trombone and Pat a flute with several pads missing from its keys.

"How is it going at the Rheingold Brewery?" Helen asked Peggy.

"God willing, and the creek do sink, Pickles may have work or he may not," Peggy answered in one of her trademark riddles, using her husband's well-known nickname. Peggy searched the band to make sure she could see her strawberry blond children known as the Gherkins; young Maggie carried a guitar and young Tommy a tin whistle.

"Governor Edwards vowed New Jersey would not pass that amendment," said Kitty as she put down a kitchen chair between her two friends. "It will put too many people out of work."

Kitty's children and granddaughter had followed her out of the house, and were finding their place in the parade formation. Frank, as usual, was the bandleader, choosing the songs for the annual extravaganza. Even though this decades-long tradition had started when they were his niece's age, as adults they decided to keep the twice yearly musical spectacles going because of the solidarity and continuity it provided the next generation of Liberty Street families.

Pete carried a snare drum, Lil a tarnished trumpet, and Doris a sparkling triangle. They joined Marvin Solomon who waved to his mother sitting next to Helen Smith. Gripped in each fist were wooden *ra'ashans*. When Marvin waved, the noisemakers spun, setting off a terrific clatter. Jim Ryan often teased Marvin about the Solomons being one of the lost tribes of Ireland. Not only had the Solomons come from Manhattan to the Oranges as Jim did, but Marvin had managed to get enlisted in the Fighting 69th of the 42nd Rainbow Division, the Irish heritage unit of the New York National Guard. So fierce had Marvin been in battle, not only earning a medal for valor, but also with his passionate yell of the unit's battle cry *Garryowen and Glory!* that his fellow Guardsmen christened him "Murph".

Mrs. Solomon smiled. Standing next to Murph was his sister Barbara, draped in a sousaphone Mike Smith had found for her in the trash behind Edison's recording laboratory. Hirsh Solomon had to work this Saturday, so his wife was happy to keep company with her neighbors and enjoy the happily raucous music festival that always marked this March afternoon. She leaned over towards the other women.

"The governor is a man of his word. He did see to it that the legislature in Trenton ratified the 19th Amendment."

"How many more to go until all the women in America get the right to vote?" asked Mrs. Jablonski, who had sat down on Peggy's left. Her buxom, blonde daughters both answered to the name of Stash, as did her husband. They were Orthodox Christians who usually celebrated Easter around the same time as Purim and St. Patrick's Day. As maestro, Frank Dodd always made room for the comely accordion-playing sisters.

"I don't know," Kitty admitted. "But it was quite a feat getting our men to get their Essex County representatives to fall in line and vote for it this time. Remember back in 1915 when they voted against it? I told my son-in-law that he'd better use whatever persuasion he had if he was going to give his baby girl a more equal life than his mother was presently enjoying."

All the women laughed. They knew Kitty had been looking out for her only grandchild, even before the tragic loss of Mariah. After that death, Kitty's advocacy of a better future for Doris was a way to turn her sorrow into a more constructive emotion.

"We're going to get the vote before our sisters do in Ireland," Kitty said to Peggy. "You mark my words."

Kitty waved to the housewives across Liberty Street, sitting on similar chairs and benches, waiting for the parade to start. In another seven months it would be the street's annual Columberfest. Mr. DiNicholangelo always launched the fall parade by uncorking his latest vintage from the maze of Tuscan grape trellises he nurtured behind the family's house. Mr. DiNic's son and daughter-in-law, Danny and Millie Paris, sat on either side of the wizened Italian émigré; he spoke no English, so they had to translate everything for him. Nobody asked questions about the difference in last names. Danny and Millie waved back to Kitty as their three children stepped into the street with their instruments. Sonny carried a saxophone; Marie, a piccolo, and Junior a pair of spectacularly dented cymbals.

Then Al and Barbara Leinhart, another immigrant family, this one from Alsace Lorraine in France, arrived at the parade's staging ground. The couple had five daughters and two were pulling the family's rickety glockenspiel, an unwieldy band instrument made of wood whose wheels were always threatening to fall off. A third sister, Clara, held the padded mallets. Marie was running scales to warm up her old clarinet and Lorraine was clearing out the spit in her French horn.

Frank Dodd surveyed the colorful, motley crew. He knew he was missing a couple of key members to complete the grandiosely named Rue de Liberté Philharmonic Marching Orchestra. Just then the Tierneys showed up. Frank wryly noted Mrs. Tierney had a chair and an umbrella to protect her from the March sun. Her husband Andrew, who like her had come to the Oranges from Pert, Scotland by way of Newark, and son Elton brought the orchestra's crowning instruments, a magnificent pair of bagpipes. Father and son also were dressed to the nines in tartan kilts from their Scottish clan.

Frank could practically feel all the young ladies of Liberty Street swoon at Elton's bare, muscular legs. At six-foot-five, Elton often worked in the family's yard with his shirt off, his washboard abdomen like nectar for bees. The girls found any excuse they could invent to wander down to the Tierney property and strike up a conversation with Elton. Even the soft burr of a faint Highland accent could cause them to visibly glow. A friendly rivalry between Elton, Frank and Pete kept the social scene lively among these highly eligible young ladies.

Frank started waving his baton, and silence descended. He raised both arms and all the musicians shuffled to attention. On the down beat they began with an inventive adaptation of the traditional Purim prayer, *Shoshanat Yaakov*, always sung to a popular tune. Frank chose one of his favorite Broadway melodies, *When Irish Eyes Are Smiling,* for this year's rendition. And, as usual, he switched up the order, having the band play the closing prayer song as the opener.

The crowd lining Liberty Street burst into spontaneous applause! Frank bowed. The musicians bowed. They bowed to the crowd. They bowed to each other. Frank then summoned his sister for her solo. Looking over at her husband and mother, Lil smiled, threw back her head to sweep her hair away from her face, and sang with fierce passion an Irish rebel song her parents had taught her:

When I was a young girl, their marching and drilling
Awoke in the glenside sounds awesome and thrilling
They loved poor old Ireland, to die they were willing
Glory O, Glory O, to the bold Fenian men.

Hoots and hollers followed. Kitty and Jim blew Lil kisses. The afternoon thus unfolded, alternating between instrumental numbers and those sung as solos, duets, and in acapella harmonies. For the finale Frank chose a popular ragtime number he'd picked up when he got out of the Navy. The band ran through the chorus and then everyone joined in from the sheets Frank had had typed with the words:

Saloon, saloon, saloon.
Have you been forgotten so soon?
You nestled so sweet in that little side street,
So respected, protected by cops on the beat.
Since you've left us the world seems in darkness,
like a cloud passing over the moon.
No more joys in my life, no more lies to my wife.

In a sweet Irish tenor Frank sang the second verse:

I can picture swinging doors wide open.
I can almost see the sawdust on the floor.
And I dream of pals and cronies drinking highballs, steins and ponies,
I can see the name of "Ehret" on the door.
But the free lunch counter now is but a mem'ry,
It has vanished with the joys we used to know.
Never more we'll hear that old familiar parting:
Just one drink, boys, just one more, before we go.

The Liberty Street denizens erupted in whoops, catcalls, shouts of glee, and holiday salutations for St. Patrick, Purim, and Easter. The good cheer of infectious, uplifting, just-plain feel-good emotions trumped the March breeze chilling the air. With the sun descending on the rim of Pleasant Valley, the afternoon's performance came to a close.

But Kitty Dodd had one surprise up her sleeve for the family's return to their house. In the kitchen she handed Doris tumblers for each place setting. As the adults gathered around the spicy corned beef and cabbage dinner, waiting ceremoniously for Kitty to join them, they were startled to see her enter the dining room with an unfamiliar pitcher in her hands. A small smile played at her lips, her only giveaway. This was her family and she wasn't intending to keep secrets from them, though she had since that week in January when she bought a double bag of potatoes and extra sugar from Jimmy Jimmy.

"I've figured out a way to make us all a steady living."

Chapter 3: The Ax Falls

It might have been too warm day to hold a tea party, but Kitty didn't care. She wasn't intending to serve a hot liquid this August afternoon. In the months following the reveal of the clear *poitin* that she had finally figured out how to distill evenly on a gas stove instead of a peat fire, Kitty's family had been quietly selling the alcohol in pint-size Ball jars to various friends and acquaintances outside their Liberty Street circle. Even John Monteverdi had tried the brew, and approved of its quality, much to Kitty's delight.

But the satisfaction Kitty received from watching her family's finances slowly improve was tempered by the very real possibility that New Jersey might go dry. Kitty watched with dismay as her best friend's family struggled to make ends meet. Tom McNichols was dangerously close to losing his job as a Rheingold delivery driver. Like other breweries, wine distributors, and bars throughout the state and elsewhere, Rheingold's management hadn't come up with any kind of strategy to stop the gathering momentum of temperance leaders and the Anti-Saloon League which continued, state by state, to get the federal amendment ratified.

Three days ago, though, women had been given the right to vote. Passage of the 19th Amendment to the Constitution on August 20, 1920 called for a celebration, Kitty decided. Unknown to the ladies who had responded to Kitty's invitation, this social tea was to be a coming-out party.

In an antsy mood, Frank and Pete could barely pay attention to Kitty's request to place the dining room chairs around the living room furniture, counting to make sure every mother would have a place to sit. Their pent-up excitement over becoming the proud owners of a Model T Ford, albeit second-hand, made them useless for any additional chores. Kitty shooed her sons out of the house, and their brother-in-law gladly joined them. Eagerly, the three men took off for parts unknown to road test the brothers' new prized possession.

Before too long, the ladies started to arrive and Lil greeted them at the door. With a brand-new cream-colored Lenox teapot she could now afford to buy, Kitty entered the living room, causing the gathered women to stop gabbling, in part, because they noticed she held the vessel in her bare hands.

"Kitty, now, you can lead a horse to hot water," started in Peggy, "but you have to look in his mouth."

"Oh," Lil said, "Mother's going to serve cold tea."

The women looked quizzically at Kitty and Lil.

"I'll pour for whoever is curious," said Kitty. A small smile teased at the corners of her mouth; she knew her offer would pique their interest.

Immediately Peggy held out her cup and saucer. "I know you've disappeared up the gopher hole in your Alice blue gown, and I've got to follow you."

Not to be outdone, other cups were quickly held aloft for Kitty to pour a genteel amount into the delicate bone porcelain that matched the Lenox teapot. Only Mrs. Solomon paused to see if she could recognize any scent from the unknown liquid before taking a sip. Peggy, Millie Paris, Helen Smith, Barbara Leinhart, and Mrs. Jablonski didn't think twice: they tossed back their cups' contents. Barbara coughed softly as the fermented potato water tickled the back of her throat.

"Why Kitty Dodd!" exclaimed Peggy. "You've made Irish moonshine!

Kitty's smile broadened, pleased by Peggy's recognition and their shared Irish heritage.

"Yes, it's pronounced *potcheen*," Kitty explained, "the Irish Water of Life. And you ladies can make it, too. Now that the 19th Amendment passed, I think the time has come to liberate our purses from poverty!"

The women broke out in excited chatter.

Kitty leaned forward in her chair, and as they quieted down, she explained how they could help their husbands make more money for their families. First, they would order copper pots used to humidify rooms and small Ball jars in bulk from Sears, Roebuck. Then, they would place a quantity order for potatoes with Jimmy Jimmy's new wholesale grocery business. Sugar and yeast, too. They had plenty of water from the municipal supply that came into their homes. With their steam-fitting skills, the Dodd boys would reroute dedicated gas lines to each home from their own house with a switch so the meters wouldn't register any increase in energy at the various houses. The ladies were free to sell their batches of *poitin* anywhere they wouldn't compete with one another.

"But what about Mrs. Tierney?" asked Mrs. Jablonski. The women turned their heads, looking for the one missing housewife and mother among them. Indeed, Mrs. Tierney was noticeably not at Kitty's 19th Amendment Tea Party.

"She's campaigning to get our state legislators to pass the 18th Amendment," Lil noted, dryly.

"What if she's…," Barbara stopped in mid-sentence as a larger realization dawned. "What if the nation goes completely dry?"

The question hung in the air.

"Well!" Millie huffed, "We'll just have to find a way to buy her cooperation."

That proposition caused a new round of chatter.

"To get anywhere, she has to go on foot, even when she's campaigning door to door," Kitty said after a while. "When the family goes to church, they have to walk. Now that Jimmy Jimmy doesn't come around, Andrew and Elton have to bring the groceries home by hand."

"Well, now, how 'bout we just buy her a car?" Peggy offered wryly.

"It doesn't have to be brand new," added Helen, taking Peggy's suggestion seriously. "If we make enough selling this *poitin* we could buy something second-hand. Didn't you, Kitty? My son can fix up Mrs. Tierney's car to look like new. He can fix yours up, too.

"You should look at what he did with his second-hand Chevrolet Ton Truck," Helen continued with obvious pride over her recently acquired knowledge about Detroit and her son's World War I talent. "It was only two years old, but beat up all to heck, and already rusting. He swapped out the bad metal, added new chrome, lacquered the whole shebang cherry red, and trimmed it out in black. It looks like new.

"Why, if we started making this *poitin,* he could trade a couple of pints for some brand new Firestone white-wall tires."

Kitty smiled to herself. Her initial assumption was correct: for the plan to work, all the families on Liberty Street had to have a grub stake in it. Nothing got past any of these women. Before too long, she'd be hearing judgmental comments from Mrs. Tierney about her sons' "new" automobile to say nothing of someone noticing the two 50-gallon fermenting tanks Frank and Pete had converted from rain barrels and placed behind the house. They were dumping the potato mash into Edison's Brook that ran behind all the houses on the east side of Liberty Street. More *poitin* production would mean it would only be a matter of time until another family saw the milky white residue, or worse, smelled it, and started asking the Dodds questions.

Best to nip three buds with one bush, if Kitty could correctly predict Peggy's advice.

Eager to get started after the 19th Amendment Tea Party, several women hadn't waited for Sears, Roebuck to deliver their orders. On that following Monday they organized a sortie to Dempsey's Hardware Store in the Oranges. Borrowing against their husband's paychecks, they bought out all the copper pots and coils Clarence Dempsey had in stock.

"Ye gods and little fishes!" cried Mr. Dempsey. "I'm cleaned out. Do I need to order more for you?"

Others went down the street to Monteverdi's and cleaned out the week's supply of potatoes, yeast, and all his confectionary. They, too, borrowed against their husband's pay. Once home, they cobbled together homemade stills for their stovetops from the utensils they already had. In another couple of weeks, boxes from Sears, Roebuck began arriving on doorsteps up and down Liberty Street, and the next group of ladies trooped down the hill to Monteverdi's, and again emptied his shelves of sugar and yeast, and the wooden boxes where he displayed his potatoes.

In the nights and weekends that followed, Frank, Pete, Elton, Mike, and Murph rolled up their sleeves and began assembling the assorted hardware and lumber in kitchens and backyards on both sides of Liberty Street. Depending on what each housewife had bought, ordered, or was able to handle, each set-up was different, posing problems that wouldn't become clear until months into the secret operation.

At Kitty's suggestion, Elton made his mother understand that he had a part-time job with the Dodds, helping them set up and maintain the fermenting barrels and stove-top cookers at each neighbor's house. Times were tough with not enough factory jobs to go around and unemployment lines growing longer, he pointed out. Being paid in pints of *poitin* that he could then sell in their former Newark neighborhood helped bring extra cash home to the Oranges. Morally torn but financially pinched, Mrs. Tierney agreed to look the other way.

It took some time to get start, but before too long, Kitty and her sorority of Liberty Street housewives were earning almost as much as the men who were working long hours at half pay just to hold on to the factory jobs they had. After settling their accounts at Dempsey's and Monteverdi's, the ladies eventually cleared enough in profits to buy a Ford coupe for Mrs. Tierney. With whitewall tires! As part of his contribution to the neighborhood-wide recognition of Mrs. Tierney's cooperation, Mike Smith painted the sporty vehicle a fetching shade of sapphire blue.

Though she couldn't drive, her son did, and Mrs. Tierney could be seen sitting in the rumble seat as Elton chauffeured her up Liberty Street for Sunday worship and assorted social calls. More obvious still, Mrs. Tierney looked straight ahead on her weekly excursions out of the neighborhood, and Kitty and the rest of the ladies breathed a collective sigh of relief. Naturally, Elton could also be seen in the Ford coupe squiring the lovely younger ladies of Liberty Street on various soirees without anyone sitting in the mother-in-law seat, but that is a story for another time.

By the time Trenton legislators ratified the 18th Amendment to the U.S. Constitution on March 9, 1922, potato mash was piling up in Edison's Brook. The mild winter hadn't produced enough snow on top of the Watchung Range to wash the smelly residue down stream. Doris, maturing into a proper young lady, had begun to complain of the growing stench. Kitty knew they had to find a solution. Fortunately, it wasn't long in coming.

"Here," Mike Smith said, setting down two quarts. "This here's the sweet apple cider for Doris. This other's the hard stuff for the adults."

He winked at Kitty. In his truck parked at his parents' house he had more of the fermented cider he had traded his *poitin* for. While his father gave his son, daughter and even wife approval to make small batches of *poitin*, Mr. Smith was still pursuing his patent lawsuit against Thomas Edison and didn't want any distractions that would take him away from proving his legitimate claim to a new way of making molded plastic. If he won, he could re-open his tool-and-dye business, hire his mechanically gifted son, and move the family back to Glen Ridge.

"Mike," asked Kitty, in a causally off-handed manner. "What are we going to do about all that mash out back?"

Mike paused, scratching his forehead above his left eye.

"We might have the solution right here," he said, nodding at the two quarts sitting on her kitchen table. "Let me see what I can find out the next time I go back up to Dowd Farms."

Two weeks later, Mike returned to the Dodds' house, not on

foot this time, but driving his truck. He backed it down the alley. Murph Solomon was with him. The two men got out with shovels in their hands. Frank and Pete came out the back door to join them while Kitty stood at the top of the stoop.

"Figure it will take us a couple of weeks, doing a little bit every day," Mike was explaining. He swung around and looked up at Kitty.

"Turns out American pigs like this slop as much as Irish pigs must have back in Cork," he teased. "Dowd said he'd be happy to fatten his like they do in the old country.

"They'll make a funny sight once they've had their fill of the Liberty Street mash," Mike added.

"Oh," Kitty started, then immediately smiled with both understanding and approval: of course, the swine. She had had her fill of eating *crubeens* growing up; salted pigs' feet, just like all pork, was food for the poor. They were working hard to never be poor in America.

"Glory be to God that Mr. Dowd agreed to take the mash," she said.

But the mash removal was only a temporary solution to what was turning out to be a much larger problem. It wasn't just that the ladies had gone from buying their potatoes at Monteverdi's market to ordering them wholesale from Jimmy Jimmy. The process itself was hugely cumbersome. All that peeling, dicing, fermenting, and then hauling the boiled mash down to dump in Edison's Brook. For the families across the street, it took twice as long to make the trek to the stream with bucket after bucket of cooked potato pulp.

As Kitty went inside, she muttered to herself, "Next time I see John Monteverdi, I'll buy a small bag of rye grain. Let's see what Da's homebrewed whiskey recipe tastes like in the Oranges."

As the ink dried on the 18th Amendment, saloons all over the Garden State began to close. Bar backs were dismantled and put in storage. Breweries, which ironically had sided with the Women Christian Temperance Union to thwart passage of the 19th Amendment, now found themselves out of business unless they wanted to make two percent beer. Thousands of employees were let go. Tom McNichols was one of the fortune few to get rehired by Rheingold as a combination janitor and night watchman but for a fraction of the pay he had had as a delivery driver.

Ironically, even as Prohibition closed down once-legitimate businesses, illegal ones sprung up to take their place. To borrow a page from Colm Kelleher's playbook, they had to hide in plain sight to be successful. Perhaps no location was more ideal than Elizabeth's waterfront. It was a maze of Central Jersey railroad tracks and box cars forever unloading and reloading, plus piers for commercial ships and fishing trawlers, and the yards for building them. On a side road known by only those in the know, Elizabeth's most famous madam, Ali DeCastro, operated a warehouse she had inherited from her dear, departed Tony. Only she didn't use it for storage.

Using the code name of Lobster Lil, the short, peroxide blond operated a speakeasy where guests with the right calling cards could get anything they wanted: liquor, opiates, women, men, high-stakes card games, fresh seafood, cargo that just happened to fall off the ships, and an occasional evening of song whenever the piano player showed up. Sometimes the joint even featured fan dancers. Lobster Lil's closest rival was Texas Guinan, Manhattan's notorious nightclub doyenne. Jim Ryan had tipped off his brothers-in-law to Lobster Lil's, thinking it would be an ideal location to sell Kitty's new batch of Irish rye whiskey.

On the last Friday of the month, Frank and Pete loaded up the

Ford sedan with every bottle of rye and a few extra bottles of *poitin* for good luck and headed due east.

"Ask for Big Dan Leonard," Jim told them. "He's the dock foreman who's on door duty this month. The password is *ramshorn*."

Jim also knew Dan loved to talk about boxing. He was certain Frank and Dan would quickly establish common ground, and Kitty's rye would find steady customers.

"Don't forget about trading for Scotch or rum," Jim added. "We could branch out what we sell here in the Oranges."

The parking lot was packed when Frank and Pete arrived. Lobster Lil had a celebrity guest in the house, the noted rum runner Bill McCoy's girlfriend and famed ladylegger in her own right, Cleo Lythgoe. Frank was smitten instantly by the sound of her smoky alto when Dan Leonard opened the hatch in the door.

Good-bye boys, I'm through,
Each one that I have met.
I say good-bye to you
And leave without regret.

I'm through and all flirtation
Has no more fascination
Good-bye boys, good-bye boys,
Good-bye boys, I'm through.

Pete elbowed his brother.

"Ramshorn," Frank said, then added for good measure as he held up a bottle of rye and a bottle of *poitin*, "Jim Ryan sent us."

Big Dan grinned broadly, and let the brothers in.

"Who's the snake charmer?" Frank asked, eager to try out the slang he was picking up.

"That's the real McCoy's Bahama Queen," Leonard said. "She's here paying her respects to Lobster Lil and trading us a few bottles of English Scotch and island rum. What do you have for us?"

Stepping into an alcove, Frank and Big Dan negotiated terms for a steady cash exchange for Kitty's homemade brands that included a small quantity set-aside for trade of any imported liquor. About to turn his shift over to the midnight doorman, Dan invited Frank to join him for a plate of raw clams. Pete disappeared into the crowd to see if he could find anybody he knew.

Because the warehouse was so large and crowded, neither brother noticed the tall, solitary figure with the busted nose standing off to one side. Jock Sanders' steel-gray eyes drew a bead on Pete and followed him until he got lost in the throng of women with bobbed hair gaily dancing with lawyers, cops, politicians, businessmen, prosecutors, and members of the clergy who had left their collars back at the rectory.

"The only thing I love more than boxing is cars," Big Dan said after a while. "There's a fresh round of exotic models coming out of Detroit later this year. In fact, we've got a brand-new prototype sitting on the loading dock. It didn't come from Detroit, but do you want a look-see?"

Frank could hardly contain himself. Like Dan, he loved cars. While Henry Ford stuck to his plain black Model Ts, his Detroit competitors were unveiling snazzy vehicles with new features year after year. It was the 20th century's heyday of style and automotive technology.

"As a matter of fact, I'm afraid to even show it to you," Leonard added. "It's going out tomorrow on the *Highland Queen*."

The pair walked out an unmarked side door that opened onto a dock stacked with cargo. Leonard yanked off a canvas tarp already stamped and strapped for shipment. Gleaming yellow with red detailing, the long, low-slung beauty designed by LeBaron Carrossiers of Bridgeport, Connecticut, had two spare whitewall tires mounted like cabochons on either side of the chassis. Big, luscious leather seats and burl wood for the dashboard complemented the interior. It sat eight. To boot, it was a convertible. Frank almost fainted.

"It's going to Cork, Ireland."

Frank quickly recovered. "My mother's from there."

They scrutinized the export documents and bills of lading. The customer was Lord Marcus Reifer.

"I know that name, that son of a bitch is one of the English landlords in Ireland," Frank said. "I was in my teens before I realized 'damn Brits' was two words, that's how much we hate them."

"Well," Leonard said, scratching his chin, a glint in his brown eyes, "even though all the paperwork is done, we could send another car."

Frank almost fell down. "I have just this car" he said, quickly offering to exchange the Dodds' Ford.

As Frank removed the license plates, Leonard siphoned the gasoline from the Ford into the LeBaron. Next, using two-by-fours to make it look as large as the Packard it was replacing, the men rewrapped the sedan. The finishing touch was to put the hoist strings in place so the cargo would be ready for loading first thing in the morning.

A couple of hours later, as Lobster Lil was closing her club before dock workers began arriving for the early morning shift, Pete joined Frank outside in the parking lot.

"What happened to the Model T?" Pete asked.

"I had it painted."

"Look, it's three times as big as the Ford…" Pete's voice trailed off as he bent his head to the ground, trying to shake the grin from his face. Pete couldn't be mad at Frank if he tried.

But clearly they faced a conundrum. The LeBaron was too wide for their narrow alley-turned-driveway. Then there was the bright yellow paint that made the Packard stand out in sharp relief against the drab gray wood of Liberty Street houses. And finally, there was Kitty's reaction to consider.

"Ma's going to pitch a fit," Pete predicted as they coasted up to the curb in front of their home. The kitchen light was on. To be sure, it was early for anyone to be stirring. After John Dodd's death, though, Kitty never got out of the habit of fully sleeping whenever any members of the family were out late.

"What do we have here, gentlemen?" Kitty asked as she opened the front door just as they climbed the steps.

"Oh, we have a surprise for you, Ma," Pete said, not sure how to bridge the divide between Frank's unbelievable stroke of luck at Lobster Lil's and their mother's certain disapproval of the flashy, brand-new family car. How could they hide this hulking vehicle in plain sight?

But to his surprise, and secret relief, Kitty did take notice of how much Frank was over the moon about the shiny and elegant prototype. That it had been destined to go to Lord Reifer's son sealed its new ownership with the Dodds.

"Here's what you're going to do," Kitty began. "Go see Mike Smith over at Edison's paint shop and get him to tone it down."

"Then what?" Pete asked, knowing that the touring car's size was still a problem.

"Then you're going to go make an offer to the nice young man Richard Codey who just opened up that new funeral parlor in town," Kitty continued. "Tell Mike to give your, ah, acquisition a sedate black color. A car like that will lend class to any cortege."

Kitty was right, but not quite in the conservative fashion she had decreed. When Mike finished, the LeBaron gleamed with black lacquer and its former red detailing was exchanged for an elegant silver accent.

But she had accurately sized up young Mr. Codey's eagerness to launch his new business with some panache. Dick agreed to store the car in one of his garages in exchange for its use for funerals and the occasional wedding rental. The Dodds would have access to it any time they wanted to take a drive, no questions asked.

Kitty pulled two heavy iron skillets out of her oven. Marked with the sign of the cross to let the devil escape, the tops of her soda bread were crowned with a fine brown crust. John Monteverdi would be happy to get this batch to sell to his afternoon customers, plus the new pints of *poitin* cooling on the back stoop. As she set the skillets on the stove top to cool, Kitty glanced out her kitchen window and noticed a man dressed in formal coveralls tapping a metal rod at regular intervals to the ground in front of him. Slowly, he was working his way from the curb down the alley.

This won't do, Kitty said to herself.

Hurriedly she smoothed back some stray hairs from her face, inadvertently spreading left-over flour across her cheekbones. Kitty ran to the front door, pulled it open and called out in a firm voice.

"May I help you?"

Startled, the man turned around. Kitty noticed the letters of the utility company embroidered on the front of his work clothes, PSE&G. The man fumbled and took out an identification card and handed it to Kitty.

"Oh, I'm sorry. I didn't realize anyone was home. I would have come to the door and knocked."

The card identified him as Edward Crump, a PSE&G field representative. Kitty breathed a small sigh of relief. This man wasn't with the law. But he was with the gas company, and that posed a different problem. Kitty fixed her blue eyes at the inspector and gave him a warm smile.

"Mr. Crump, I'm just about to put a pot on for tea," she said. "I've taken some fresh soda bread out of the oven. Would you care to come in and join me?"

Surprised, Mr. Crump looked almost apologetic.

"I don't want to trouble you. No. It's not necessary."

"Please, I insist. No trouble at all. With all the hard work you've been doing, I'm sure a good strong cup of tea would be welcomed right now. Come in." Kitty motioned to the open front door and made her smile more encouraging as though she were talking to her granddaughter. Enchanted, the company man responded, climbing the steps of the front porch.

"Right this way, Mr. Crump. Why don't you sit yourself down here at the dining room table. This is the best seat here by the window." Kitty silently thanked the Holy Father that the dining room was opposite the kitchen, its windows overlooking the other neighbor's alley. "I'll just go put on the water. Make yourself comfortable. Will butter be all right for your bread?"

In about five minutes Kitty bustled back into the dining room with a serving tray loaded with the older chipped teapot she had stored in a cupboard, two plain mugs, a small cracked dish with butter, and slices from the last loaf of bread she had just pulled from the oven.

"Now what seems to be the problem?" Kitty asked as she filled his cup. "We pay our bills."

"Oh, no, it's not that," Mr. Crump responded, lathering butter on the slice of bread Kitty handed him. "You must be Mrs. Dodd."

"Yes, I'm Kitty Dodd."

"Well, I'm here checking for gas leaks," he began. "They're very dangerous, gas leaks are. They can lead to explosions or asphyxiations. No telling what can happen. According to our records, you're using four times what you did this time last year."

He stopped his explanation to comment on the taste of the freshly baked soda bread. "Oh, this is wonderful. Just like my grandmam used to make it."

Crump, Edward Crump, Kitty racked her memory of families in Ireland.

"I knew some Crumps up in Roscommon," said Kitty, thickening her brogue. "But you wouldn't be with that clan."

"No, my folks were from Meath."

"No, no those Crumps were all hung for sheep stealing," replied Kitty with a twinkle in her eyes. "You couldn't be those Crumps."

Mr. Crump chuckled, finding himself at ease with the sounds and memories of his Irish upbringing.

"Well, Mr. Crump," said Kitty, "We are paying for the gas, aren't we?"

"Oh yes," he responded.

Kitty got quiet and took out a handkerchief to dab at her eyes. Quietly, she began to sob.

"Is there something wrong Mrs. Dodd?"

"Mr. Crump, I don't know how to tell you this. I'm somewhat ashamed but things have not been going well for my family in Ireland and we have to send everything we can make to help them out. To do that my family bought used laundry equipment from the Orange Memorial Hospital. It was industrial size, and we are doing the laundry for the Edison workshop. It helps make the extra money needed back home. I'm ashamed to tell people we've stooped so low to have to do this."

Edward Crump looked with new eyes at Kitty.

"No, no, you're an honest working woman, you shouldn't be

ashamed," he jumped in. "You should be proud of taking on extra work to help your family back home in Ireland. That explains the extra gas."

"I'm not doing anything illegal, am I Mr. Crump?"

"Oh no, you should be credited, God bless you, Mrs. Dodd!"

With that, Mr. Crump pushed back his chair and picked up his hat. "I will inform the home office in Newark."

Kitty smiled across her handkerchief as she finished dabbing at her eyes.

"Why, thank you Mr. Crump. Let me wrap the rest of the soda bread for you to take home. And God bless you, Mr. Crump."

Kitty made a mental note to send Edward Crump a card at Christmas time.

"Okay, I've got to admit, I'm not the world's best cook," Mrs. Jablonski said. "Distilling fermented potato water isn't my cup of tea, if you get what I'm saying."

She looked at Peggy McNichols.

"I like the money, but the work is hard and the quality isn't always consistent," she added. "I've been hearing stories from my Polish relatives in Jersey City that people can go blind if the alcohol isn't made right."

Mrs. Jablonski inhaled deeply and exhaled loudly.

"And I don't think I'm the only Liberty Street housewife that gets a batch returned because it doesn't taste right... You're Kitty's best friend. Can you talk to her?"

Peggy stood up, absorbing all of what Mrs. Jablonski said.

"All right. I'll ask."

Later that afternoon, Peggy and Kitty sat in the Dodd's kitchen as the day's final loaves of bread baked in the oven.

"Old habits are hard to break," Kitty said, looking at her new wrist watch to see how much longer before the loaves were finished. "Mr. Monteverdi's Friday customers have gotten so used to having my bread to take home for dinner that's it's hard to give up baking them."

"Kitty," Peggy paused before plunging into a rush of words she hoped would sound logical and persuasive, "what would you say to having the Dodd family take over the whole *poitin* operation? Maybe figuring out some way to divvy up the labor among all the families on Liberty Street, but to have you be in charge of the cooking? So the moonshine is uniform?"

Kitty was somewhat taken aback, unaware that her friends had encountered any difficulty. "Why didn't they come to me?"

"Well, they were afraid to ask you directly, being as you set them up with instructions and didn't ask for any money in return for your idea," Peggy explained. "They're overwhelmed with the amount of work. Besides, we need a leader, Kitty. We can't all be equals. Even the suffragists had leaders."

Kitty was silent for a moment. "Okay, let me talk it over with my family."

That night at dinner, Kitty laid out the simple request of the ladies of Liberty Street.

"It stands to reason," started in Frank. "Every house gets a big delivery of potatoes. Some use sugar. Some use molasses. Some, brown sugar. Some, honey."

He held up his left hand, bending down a finger with each point he made.

"Then, every house has to clean those outside fermentation barrels with bleach or lye every time a new batch of potatoes goes in." Another finger went down.

"Everyone has to dump the mash into the brook, twice the distance for everyone living on the west side of the street."

He paused.

"But most of all, I bet everyone distills at a different temperature. Mike found that out trying to make an outdoor still he fed with wood for fire. It was hard to keep the temperature even until the distilling was done."

Kitty looked in wonder at her son who had dropped out of St. John's grammar school at the same time as his older brother. The two had strung together an assortment of odd jobs from delivering newspapers, sweeping sidewalks, and hauling little old ladies' groceries up tenement stairs until they found relatively steady jobs at Sam McGee's gym where they traded part of their hourly pay for training to be boxers. Frank's ability to evaluate a production cycle and find its inefficiencies came as a revelation to Kitty.

"I'm not sure about staying with *poitin*," she began. "The potato mash is getting to be a bother, especially to get rid of it. In that new barrel you built me, the sour rye mash produces half the amount of residue because we use it twice. But even running it once to make sweet mash still produces less than the potatoes we dump in the brook. Plus, we are getting more money for the whiskey," she added.

"I think cutting over to rye will take less time and will be less obvious to outsiders. So, if we did take over the entire operation, and switch to making whiskey, how would we distribute the money?" Kitty asked, looking around the table.

Jim pulled a notepad from the breast pocket of his suit coat. "Give me a little time and I'll figure out a fair share for everyone."

Kitty got up and moved to the stove from where she couldn't resist adding, "Make the figures work so your wife can quit that damn radium factory job once and for all."

Jim nodded in agreement. His daughter Doris jumped up from her chair and ran over to kiss her father's cheek and put her arms around his neck in a hug. Lil smiled from across the table. Wouldn't it be good to leave that factory job for a family business the Dodds could manage and make more money, to boot?

"You know," said Jim, as he continued to work the numbers, "if we buy an empty warehouse or some old abandoned factory so we can expand our production and make more, we could open up new markets by dealing in cased goods rather than individual bottle sales."

Kitty stopped preparing the after-dinner tea and turned around to look her son-in-law with new-found respect. "We could close down all these outdoor kitchen operations, couldn't we? And not worry about any gas agents sniffing around?"

"Or any Treasury agents," Jim said.

"Yes," exclaimed Frank and Pete in unison.

"Explain to me those figures whenever you're ready," Kitty added.

The next day Kitty outlined the new plan to Peggy.

"We'll buy all the materials and maintain the cookers," she said, "in return for earning the largest percentage.

"Every family that works will receive two dollars an hour, regardless of who works," she continued. "The women get to choose who will represent their families.

"If the operation gets really big, more family members will be able to work. And you'll be able to take home some whisky to sell to your steady customers," Kitty added.

"Oh my God," Peggy gasped, "that was more than the women were even thinking about."

Inwardly Kitty thought to herself, *What do we know about the sale and price of the real product? How are we going to find experts? And, where is there a big enough building so we can hide in plain sight?*

Chapter 4: Better Living Through Chemistry

The economic reality of Prohibition started to settle in. Factories that made glass bottles bought by distillers were forced to close while some of the hardest hit professions were those in the hospitality field. From chauffeurs to chefs, many lost well-paying jobs.

"Bet it's been a long time since you've had a home-cooked meal," Jim Ryan said, clapping his right hand on the back of his childhood friend Bill Grabowski.

As youngsters, the pair had grown up in the same tenement in Hell's Kitchen, across from the piers. Both of them were the only offspring of single mothers. But despite their rough circumstances and the constant pressure to join a gang, both boys had tougher mothers determined their sons would graduate high school and amount to something. Jim used his math skills and love of horses to get listed with the racing association as a legal bookmaker. Bill put his one and only chemistry class to the most practical use he could imagine, and became a master mixologist. He honed his talent on Coney Island at Frankie Yale's Harvard Inn for no other reason than he wanted to spend his days off at the beach with the girls.

"Remember that strawberry blonde?" Bill asked.

"And her friend we called the chocolate brunette?" Jim responded.

"That was a memorable lost weekend we spent under the boardwalk!"

"They were the days of our misspent youth."

"But to tell you the truth, even though the country's gone dry, I don't wish I was back there," Bill added.

Yale's sawdust club drew a coarse crowd. Thanks to Jim, Bill had learned of a master bartender's job at Ernest and Werner's upscale German restaurant in Jersey's Oranges. There, the clientele was more gentrified and more discerning about their liquor, too. But after the state ratified the Federal Prohibition Amendment, Bill was forced to take a lower-ranking job, with a pay cut, as the m'aître d' at the sedate, bluestocking Essex County Country Club where teetotaler Thomas Edison was a member. When Jim heard Bill had Monday nights off, he invited him to Kitty's for dinner.

"You're going to love my mother-in-law's cooking," he said. "Her coconut cake is out of this world. I think she uses chicken fat. Besides, we'll have a chance to catch up, and you'll finally meet my wife and daughter."

Once inside, and the round of introductions made, everyone but Doris settled into whiskey sour cocktails in the living room. With John Dodd gone now a little over four years, the family drank socially among trusted friends and never to excess. Kitty opened the conversation by asking Bill about his early days on Coney Island.

"The *Newark News* tells a story about an up-and-coming gangster in Chicago who came from there," she began.

"Oh, yes, that's Al Capone," Bill said, nodding in recognition.

"He switched from bouncer to bartender when I was there. Wanted to understand liquor distribution. Lots of street smarts. Very loyal to all the ethnics, so long as they're loyal to him. Heck, he even married a fair-skinned Irish girl by the name of Mae Coughlin," Bill broke off. "You know her in Ireland, Mrs. Dodd?"

Kitty shook her head.

Bill continued. "After the knife fight that gashed his face is when I decided to come to Jersey."

"Well, now," Kitty said softly, "I bet he's just misunderstood like so many men trying to make their way in a new country."

Later, as Lil and Doris cleared the dining room table and prepared to wash the dinner dishes, Kitty returned to the living room and this time sat in the room's only straight-backed chair. Realizing her son-in-law had provided her with an opportunity to learn more about the liquor business, she delicately began questioning Bill.

"Now Mr. Grabowski," she started in, "or, may I call you Billy? When you worked for Mr. Werner, what were the bar's two most popular sellers?"

"Certainly, Mrs. Dodd. Call me Billy," he responded. "Well, whiskey and gin are the two most called for."

"What brands?"

"Well, I'd have to say from Canada it's either Seagram's VO or Canadian Club for top-of-the-line rye whiskeys."

"And what about gin, Billy?"

"Well, in gin there's Gordon's, Beefeaters, and Gilbey's – all English," he pointed out. "The gin made in Cork never found favor with American drinkers."

"That's all right," Kitty said.

Bill continued, "Gilbey's is probably the most asked for gin. But either liquor that comes in from the rum runners, Mrs. Dodd, comes in their familiar bottles. Jim tells me you're selling your whiskey in

Ball jars most people use for canning."

"Yes, that's true," Kitty admitted.

"Well, if you want to ramp up production and switch to deliveries made in cases, you need to find bottles that look like the ones drinkers know."

"What are people paying?" she asked.

"Pre-Prohibition, a bottle of VO was going for fifteen, sixteen dollars," Bill said. "Now, it's upwards of twenty-five dollars, if the distributor has connections to Canada and England."

Kitty slowly nodded, taking in this information.

"Well, Mr. Grabowski, I want to thank you for coming out this evening. It seems our next level of inquiry is where to find a master distiller. You let my son-in-law know."

Bill stood up and proffered his hand to Kitty. She took it, and Bill turned the formal handshake into a gesture of extreme respect by touching his lips to the top of her hand.

Several days later, Jim walked in the door to find Kitty in the living room crocheting, a needle craft she had learned from her mother. She wanted to pass it along to Doris. While waiting for batches of *poitin* to distill on her stove, Kitty had reprised her crocheting skills.

"I heard from Bill Grabowki," Jim said slowly. "There's a distillery that's shut down... but still open...selling other products from its orchards. It's down the shore."

"Yes, and..." Kitty looked up, willing to go along with the drawn-out game.

"It's Laird & Company in Colts Neck. They've been making apple jack brandy since the colonists kicked out the British in the Revolution. Billy says the master distiller has gone back to Scotland, but the apprentice is still down there."

"Well, Jim, as Independence Day is around the corner, maybe it's high time for the family to take a little holiday," said Kitty. "I'll tell Frank to get the Packard from Mr. Codey. You tell Lil and Doris to pack an overnight bag."

Even as a Kelleher growing up in Ireland, Kitty had never been on a vacation. The money just wasn't there. As Mariah had been born shortly before John landed a job transcribing Thomas Edison's notes, and the births of Lil, Pete and Frank came so quickly and close together, that it was all the family could do to make the rent on the Liberty Street house. They had to take in a boarder until Jim Ryan came along. But now, the poverty Kitty had known for so long was lifting like a spring mist over Cork. In 1923 America's Fourth of July celebration fell right in the middle of the week. Why not take some time off and see the fabled Jersey shore she had read so much about in the *Newark Evening News?* Some time away in the fresh salt air would be good for Doris and Lil, Kitty reasoned. When Kitty brought up the idea of a seaside trip, Frank and Pete informed her there was going to be a special parade at the army training camp in Sea Girt for that July Fourth. The occasion was a celebration to honor all the veterans who had served in World War I and the Spanish-American War.

"We should go while we can still fit into our uniforms," Pete told his mother.

"We should pack some product in case opportunity presents itself," added Frank.

Jim, who had received a notice that the Coast Guard was also invited to the military reunion, nodded in agreement.

"Well, I'm not against doing a little business on the side," Kitty responded. "Just make sure you hide the product in plain sight."

Bright and early Monday morning, the Dodds and the Ryans

tucked themselves into the elegant black Packard LeBaron, its convertible top folded down, and headed for Elizabeth. From there, it was a straight shot down Route 9 to Somerville to pick up Route 7 to Freehold. Horse country. Jim Ryan knew it well.

"You'll find Laird's place in Scobeyville," he said, pointing Frank, who was driving, due east. "It's a hamlet in Colts Neck."

Nestled in an apple orchard, they found the trademark yellow shutters on the white two-story Colonial Revival home used by the Lairds as a combination house and office. Out back, the distillery was noticeably closed. A farm stand, lined with jars of applesauce and baskets filled with red and green apples tempted them from the road. Behind the stand stood a tall, robust young man, slightly balding, with a cigar clenched in the corner of his mouth.

"Might you be Bobby Browne?" Kitty asked.

The young man nodded, taking in the well-dressed individuals who were climbing out of the Packard.

"Would you like to join us for a picnic lunch? That would be alright, wouldn't it? A picnic lunch under one of the apple trees?"

The young man nodded again, surprised by his good fortune, and mystified at the same time.

Lil and Doris spread a white cloth across the grass and as Frank and Pete passed around the plates and utensils, introductions and pleasantries were exchanged, along with cold cuts and salad, until Bobby Brown lifted the veil on the family's real reason for an excursion to Laird's.

"Would it be a wild guess to say you're interested in the business yourselves?"

"Mr. Browne," Kitty started in, "has life been well since you've arrived here? Is this the job you've always dreamed of?"

"It stinks, it truly stinks!" he replied. "I didn't sign on to sell applesauce.

"Would you be interested," Kitty paused for deliberate effect, "in a career change?"

"Yes, I would! What did you have in mind?"

"How about if we pick you up next Monday on our way back from the shore? Have your bags ready and waiting for us out by the gate."

As Kitty extended her right hand to Bobby, neatly folded and tucked between her first and second fingers were five crisp $100 bills. Little did Bobby realize that in five short days he was about to embark on the career of his life.

Without looking down, Bobby said to Kitty, "I will be outside at the corner."

The Dodds and the Ryans resumed their drive along Route 7 until they picked up Route 4 south in Asbury Park. With Jim driving and Doris in the passenger seat next to him, Kitty opened a private conversation with Frank, Pete, and Lil.

"I don't like it that we're beholden to Old Tom Edison to rent his houses on Liberty Street. It's like the damn Brits all over again," she said.

"I also don't like the idea that we have so much cash in the house. I think we should put some of our money into American land, and own it instead of renting like my ancestors were forced to do in Ireland."

Frank, Pete, and Lil looked at Kitty with surprise.

"A land improvement company took out a little advertisement in the Sunday paper," Kitty said. "They are offering beach bungalows for sale in Manasquan. I think we should find one to rent for the Fourth of July and see how favorable we can make the terms."

By nightfall, the families arrived in Manasquan. At Hawes Realty they picked up keys for a seven-night beachfront rental. Driving towards the ocean, everyone breathed in deeply and acknowledged their first real vacation had officially begun.

The sun shone brightly over the parade field as veterans from all branches of the military assembled in formation for review. Kitty, Lil, and Doris sat in the stands crowded with other patriotic families who turned out to celebrate Old Glory and pay tribute to the men who had fought so valiantly for her. In addition to the veterans, the army training camp in Sea Girt was teeming with officers enlisted in training courses, plus new recruits from the state police's Wilburtha Training School who were attending a special summer boot camp. Everyone was in dress uniforms.

"Oooohhhh, so many good-looking men in uniforms," Doris swooned.

A little taken aback by her frisky daughter, Lil quickly replied, "You'll have plenty of time when you're older to think about men in uniforms!"

In charge of greeting the arriving officers, Sergeant Major Gil Gilroy of the New Jersey National Guard's 102nd Cavalry Regiment from Essex County stood at ease just as the Dodd boys strolled up to find their place in the parade formation. Right away Gil noticed there was something unique about the brothers. He peered a little closer as they drew near and noticed they had a few extra medals pinned to their Navy dress whites.

"I couldn't help admiring your awards. Where are they from?"

Looking slightly sheepish, Frank and Pete chuckled and said, "The King of Belgium pinned these on us."

By the time the Dodds finished entertaining Gil with their boxing escapades aboard the *USS George Washington,* the three men were fast friends. The brothers decided they had also made a new business contact for back home in Essex County and so invited Gil to join the family for dinner in their rental bungalow.

"Bring your bathing suit if you want a swim," Frank added.

The next night, as a golden moon rose over the Atlantic Ocean, Gil found himself on the Dodds' porch with Frank and Pete, sipping a familiar drink served in a picnic tumbler.

"I remember this!" he said. "This tastes like the real deal even though it's clear. Where did you get whiskey like this? At the camp we've lost several soldiers to poisoned alcohol. The major supplier around these quarters is Tony Two-Tone because he sometimes cuts his brew with wood alcohol. No one can tell it's a bad batch until there's been a death. The commander sees the men loitering outside the gates, trying to sell the stuff, and some of the younger ones don't know any better.

"Commandant McCabe has threatened police action, but she also knows a little liquor goes a long way to keeping the men on an even keel," he added.

"For a woman, she's one smart administrator. You know, she's the highest ranking female civilian in the military. She'd be a colonel if she was a man."

Surprised by Gilroy's revelations about the illegal alcohol problem, Frank and Pete explained the rye whiskey Gil was drinking came from their mother's Irish recipe.

"No one's ever died from our whiskey," Pete said.

Added Frank, "And we can supply you with a sample case for the camp."

Gil took another sip.

Just then Jim stepped out on the porch to join the three men.

"Sometimes the smart thing to do is go with the smaller suppliers," he said.

"A couple of weeks ago I was up at Saratoga with my good friend Buddy Keegan of Shamrock Stables. He'd invited Paddy Russo, who runs book out of Asbury Park, and Billy Northeast, the guy most consider, including himself, to be the 'King of Books' to join us.

"Now, these are the two biggest operators along the eastern seaboard. They couldn't resist digging at me for having a 'Ma and Pa operation in the Oranges'." Jim shrugged nonchalantly, slowly sipping his own glass of Kitty's whiskey.

"We all won the first race. The second race, I'm the only one who produced a winning ticket for the daily double," he paused for effect, "so they dared me to pick the winner of the third race. Buddy upped the ante, saying that the odds would double in my favor if I won. Paddy and Billy agreed to his terms."

Jim paused again for another sip.

"So I said, 'How 'bout if I pick more than one other winner?'"

By now, Jim had reeled in Gil, Frank, and Pete to his story. Kitty, who was sitting in the bungalow's front room by the open window to the porch, leaned forward, motioning to her daughter, Lil, to join her.

"The field of nine horses made the final turn and the lead horse, Ragtime, broke free of the pack and finished three lengths ahead." Jim mimicked reaching into the right pocket of his sports coat, with a flourish, feigned the winning ticket.

Lil was doing a silent calculation: a hundred dollars each from Billy Northeast and Paddy Russo. As Jim recounted his story, his winnings kept doubling. In the fourth race Jim won $200 from each man; the fifth race, $400; the sixth: $800; the seventh: $1600; the eighth: $3200; the ninth, $6400.

Impressed, Gil Gilroy, reached into his back pocket and pulled out a healthy billfold.

"How much do you want for your mother's whiskey, Frank?"

Later that night, Lil pestered her husband to give up his race-winning secret.

"Ah, my love, it was simple. I simply bought a two-dollar ticket on every horse, in every race. Every time I came back from the betting window, I kept an eye on the break-away horse and tried very hard to recall in which pocket I had put the ticket with his name on it."

He hugged his wife and kissed her.

"Would you like me to buy the family one, or two, of these bungalows?"

By Friday night Gilroy had erected a big field tent on a little used corner of the training camp. On the tent's flap he hung a sign that read:

Come see the world famous striped pig
Only one of its kind in existence
One nickel

"Are you sure this is legal?" Commander McCabe asked.

"The federal statute is all about transportation. It doesn't say consumption is illegal," Gilroy pointed out.

"Ah! A guardhouse lawyer we have here," McCabe said. "Well, we can give it try but start off small."

Several soldiers wandered over, and a few of the more adventurous found nickels in their pants pockets and paid the petty officer on guard. He lifted the tent flap and motioned them inside.

Sure enough, they were looking at an enormous sow painted with black stripes, rooting around a makeshift pen. Behind the pen that held the porcine prisoner, someone strung a khaki-colored curtain between two supporting tent poles.

"Come this way, gentlemen," Gilroy called. "There's more to see over here.

There, on the other side, was a bar, its surface lined with cups of whiskey; one to a customer at no additional charge.

Gilroy's operation went off without a hitch until Saturday night when Eddy McGinty, who was in charge of bringing in the pig from Geiser's Farm in Wall, arrived too early for the set-up. With time on his hands and Kitty's clear Irish whiskey stored under the bar, McGinty helped himself, forgetting to stripe the sow.

When Gilroy arrived at the tent, his star attraction wasn't in costume. Franticly, Gilroy looked around and noticed McGinty had passed out with his prized sunglasses still on his nose. Gingerly, Gil removed the tinted lenses and, using loose string he found, tied the glasses to the sow's snout. Then Gil used a pen to scratch "striped" from the sign and wrote in "blind". But no one seemed to notice or care whether the pig was either. The nightly nightcap at the blind pig speakeasy had become a camp ritual.

The extended Dodd family and Bobby Browne, now formerly of Laird's in Colts Neck, returned Monday to the Oranges. Thoroughly apprised of the challenges ahead, including Kitty's desire to branch out into distilling and selling gin and whiskey, Bobby spent Tuesday taking stock of each family's fermenting tanks. Methodically he noted the wildly different designs for the stovetop stills. He saw the pint-sized milk bottles were additional containers for selling whiskey and *poitin.* And, he couldn't avoid the fact that as the heat of the summer sunk in, the combined potato and rye mashes were giving off an obvious odor. That wasn't all.

"We can't use baby diapers as filters anymore. Any way we can find cheesecloth? Maybe from the Stetson hat factory?" Bobby asked of the assembled ladies, taking a well-worn cigar out of the corner of his mouth to make sure he was clearly heard.

"And we're going to need oak to build new tanks and blow

torches to char them out so we can boost the color and flavor of the whiskey," he continued.

Bobby put the nub back in the corner of his mouth, paused, took it out again, and then capped off his list of requirements with two more critical entries.

"We're going to need one large space to do all this," he said. "And, you're going to have to get real liquor bottles, not canning jars."

"We're going all the way, into the big bushes," said Peggy McNichols as she turned to Mrs. Solomon. Eager to prove they were equal to the task at hand, the two women volunteered to go in search of bottles that more accurately looked like they would contain alcohol. After all, they reasoned, the ladies could probably charge more, too, if their alcohol looked like it came in real liquor bottles.

Later that morning they took the No. 21 trolley down to Market and Broad Streets in Newark. From there they walked the remaining distance to the Newark Bottling and Glass Plant. In their handbags they separately carried samples of pre-Prohibition whiskey bottles Bill Grabowski had found for them. One was Gilbey's Gin, the other Canadian Club. The labels were steamed off. The women went and found the plant manager who was reading the *Newark News* sports pages, whiling away what was left of the morning until the automated whistle blew for lunch. They showed him their bottles.

"Do you have anything like this that we could buy?" Peggy asked.

The manager looked the women over and sighed before he turned around and disappeared into the factory. After some time passed, he returned, carrying in one hand a brown bottle with a screw cap that was an almost perfect match for the Canadian Club.

In his other hand was a clear, small bottle, also with a screw top. The original Gilbey's bottle had a metal snap top.

"Who's to say that they didn't start using the screw tops," Mrs. Solomon asked of no one in particular.

"How many do you want?"

Without pausing to ask about cost, Peggy instantly replied, "We could start out with a 100 cases of each."

"Oh," said the newly impressed manager. "Well. Sit down, ladies. Please, sit down. Let me write out your order. Could I get you some coffee? Order you some lunch?"

That evening Pat Blessington took a break from his rounds as night watchman at the Edison compound and ambled down Liberty Street to have dessert with the Dodds and their new house guest. A giant of a man, Pat was another amateur boxer from McGee's Gym who had gotten to know the Dodd brothers before they went to war.

"Oh, I've been meaning to tell you, I'm heading off to the police academy," he said, with no small degree of pride. "The Oranges Police Department has hired me. There's been a recent opening on the force. And, they're paying for my training. Friday night's my last night working for Old Tom."

Frank and Pete looked at each other and then across the table to Bobby Browne and Jim Ryan.

"Could you give us a tour of the plant?" Frank asked.

"Certainly, come back with me. We'll go now," he said. "Mrs. Dodd, thank you again for this wonderful apply barley pudding. I'll sure miss it when I'm working downtown."

Pat led Frank and Pete onto the grounds and into a shuttered building that smelled unused.

"They're not sure what they're going to do with this factory,"

Blessington said. "Mr. Edison is getting on in years. He's over eighty."

The brothers looked around. Everywhere Blessington's search light landed it picked up unused copper sheathing and tubing, temperature gauges, dials, tubs, pots of all sizes, and blow torches. With forty-eight hours left to go on the job, Pat Blessington didn't need much convincing to commandeer some industrial-sized dollies and load them with as much hardware as the brothers could wrangle out the door and down the gentle slope of Liberty Street to Kitty's backyard.

"This isn't stealing, is it boys?" she said from the kitchen door.

"Well, no," said Frank from the dark recesses of the yard. "Mr. Edison isn't using it right now. We have every intention of returning it. Perhaps in different shapes. But, no, Mother, it's not stealing."

At breakfast the next morning Jim announced that he wanted everyone to take a walk with him. Like the shepherd Kitty had so long ago said he was, Jim herded the troop from Liberty Street on a five-minute trek over to North Center Street. They were in a part of the Oranges zoned for industrial use. It included a former World War I scrap metal lot, the city's dog pound, and the public works yard which gave off a faintly rank smell. Next door to the public works stood a ramshackled property, about an acre in size, surrounded by an eight-foot wide plank fence. Weeds and debris littered the sidewalk.

"Well, Kitty," Jim said, taking a pair of keys out of his pocket, "how's this for hiding in plain sight?"

Jim unlocked the padlock on the gate and pushed it wide open. There, for everyone to see, was a one-story red brick factory, closed since the end of the war. A loading dock had been outfitted into one end of the building while an overhang to what was the front office marked the opposite side. A row of cast iron spider windows with chicken glass wire connected the two. Two smoke stacks at the rear of the roofline poked their way skyward.

"Want to see inside?"

Jim led the group over to the entrance where he inserted the second key. He swung the door open, turned to Kitty, and said, "After you."

In wonderment, Kitty walked in and promptly noted a row of offices off to one side and a factory lay-out that included a conveyor belt. She quickly appraised that under the hook-ups to the smokestacks, they could place the fermenting barrels and assorted equipment for distilling that Frank and Pete had brought home the night before.

"This will do, Jim, this will do just fine," she said with satisfaction "It fits our requirements, the price is right and the location, too."

On Friday, Frank, Pete, Al Leinhart, and Mike Smith gave notice at Thomas Edison's personnel office that they were quitting the company. Lil turned in her badge at U.S. Radium Corp. and Pickles McNichols just flat-out quit Rheingold. Monday they showed up at North Center Street joined by Elton Tierney and Murph Solomon and began retrofitting the abandoned factory, inside and out. Per Kitty's orders, they knew there would be no night work and no work on weekends. The property would be run like a legitimate business, 8 a.m. to 4:30 p.m., Monday through Friday. Kitty, Peggy, Barbara, Millie Paris, Mrs. Solomon, and Mrs. Jablonski joined the men and set about sprucing up the offices.

As usual, Frank could be counted on to serenade the Liberty Street denizens with the latest popular melody:

Yes, we have no bananas
We have-a no bananas today.
We've string beans, and onions
Cabbages and scallions,
And all sorts of fruit and say
We have an old fashioned to-mah-to
A Long Island po-tah-to
But yes, we have no bananas.
We have no bananas today.

Later that evening, Kitty and Peggy went to Millie Paris's house to have a talk with her husband.

"Now, Danny, you know we have this bottle," Kitty said, pulling out a pre-Prohibition Gilbey's Gin, its label and tax stamps still intact. "What could you do to make our new bottles look like the originals?"

"Oh, no," Danny said as he started to laugh, "I know what you're getting at Kitty… you want me to make labels!"

"Oh, wouldn't that be wonderful!" Kitty exclaimed. "We know you're such a talented printer. You and your sons could print practically anything and your artwork is superb. You should be on Madison Avenue!"

"Oh, you're buttering me up, Kitty."

While Millie Paris had joined the ladies of Liberty Street in making potcheen and then rye whiskey, Danny stayed focused with perfecting his artistic talent in design and his skill at printing. He had begun with making the labels for his father's wine bottles. As his talent and business grew, he took on more and more complex orders from stationery to business signs. One of his first corporate customers had been Jimmy Jimmy who needed signs for his new Reo delivery trucks. Danny made him a splendidly colorful sign that read "DeSeo's Produce Wholesale".

"And, Danny," added Kitty, "we're going to be needing a sign for our little operation over there on North Center Street. Could you help us with that?"

"Sure, Kitty, sure. What did you have in mind?"

Kitty smiled. "I'd like it to read 'Acme Chemical Company… Better Living Through Chemistry…Serving Home and Industry since 1893. Add Plant No. 4, Oranges, New Jersey'."

"Is that all?"

"Well, on our business cards I want just the phone number under the words 'Better Living Through Chemistry'," Kitty said. "We'll make sure Millie gets an extra case of the new batch of whiskey for your trouble."

"Make that half a case of whiskey and half a case of that new gin you're going to be selling," he responded, "and we've got a deal."

"Done."

As Kitty walked home, she recalled what Billy Grabowski had said about Al Capone. He was loyal to the immigrant class, so long as they showed allegiance to him, of course. Kitty decided Acme Chemical's delivery drivers would be newly Americanized citizens like herself with whom she had developed a mutual respect and trust. She began making a list.

"Jimmy Jimmy goes at the top," she said softly to herself. "Then the ice man, Tony Galento. It'll help pay for his son's training at McGee's Gym."

Gathering her fingers in her left hand, one at a time as she came up with names, Kitty added Mr. Becker, a Jewish immigrant who had been delivering buttermilk and other dairy products to the Dodds' doorstep since her children were babies. He was about to retire and had told Kitty he was looking for part-time work "so I won't get in my wife's way."

"If you can't trust the milkman, who can you trust?"

Approaching her front door, Kitty added one more name to the list of company contractors.

"That Reilly boy. He made good for himself and became mayor here in the Oranges. But when he was in short pants and the cops caught him, he never snitched. We can go to him for the final step before we start to ship our product."

Up until now, the families were making deliveries in fruit crates. It was obvious to anyone passing by on the street that their contents were anything but produce. The next day Kitty and Peggy paid a visit to the Reilly Box and Paper Cardboard Company in a section of the Oranges' industrial neighborhood.

"How much for making sturdy custom containers with partitions?" Kitty asked Russell Reilly.

"We need one shape for Canadian Club bottles," interjected Peggy, "and one for Gilbey's Gin."

Russ Reilly smiled and indicated it would be no problem to fabricate two different dimensions.

"And could you also make a slipcover case out of cardboard to go around the wood cases?" Kitty asked, thinking it prudent to add one more layer to Acme Chemical's hidden-in-plain-sight policy. "We really don't want to draw attention to our deliveries."

With the smile on his face broadening to a grin, Russ nodded his understanding of his new customer's requirements and was secretly thanking the Fates for this large order that came at a critical time in the company's production cycles. Like so many other manufacturers that had had contracts with Newark's breweries and distillers, business was way down.

"Sure Mrs. Dodd," he said. "We can make any kind of container you need."

As part of the negotiations, Acme Chemical would receive 200 cardboard cases at a reduced price and Russ Reilly would receive a case of each product. When all was said and done, Kitty figured it was costing them $20 to make a case of Canadian Club they could sell for $200 on the black market.

For goodwill and good measure, Kitty added, "And, Russ, I'll remember you at Christmas."

If there was anything Kitty's son Frank loved more than cars, it was the romance he associated with speakeasies like Lobster Lil's in Elizabeth and the entrepreneurial spirit he admired in Gil Gilroy's blind pig venture in Sea Girt. Nonetheless, Kitty was not happy to discover the apple hadn't fallen far from her tree of economic independence when Frank, together with Pete, informed her they were buying the vacated scrap metal yard across the street from Acme Chemical.

"Whatever for?" she asked.

"We're going to open our own place," Frank said, the excitement in his voice unmistakable.

"What?! We don't want to draw any more attention to ourselves!" Kitty's response was swift and vehement.

"No, no, it will be all right." Frank tried to sooth his mother. "We're not going to fix up the outside like we did with Acme."

"But think of all the people you might attract."

"We'll hire Tony, the ice man's son, to be a bouncer. He'll be at the door whenever he's not at McGee's," said Pete.

"I won't let you have the money from the family business for this lark," Kitty said, still somewhat angry. "You don't want to put everything at risk that we worked so hard for."

"No, no, we won't take any money from the family," Frank said. "You might say we have a private investor."

Kitty narrowed her eyes.

"And who might that be?"

"Jim offered to stake us the money to buy the place and fix it up."

Kitty shook her head, trying to clear information from her mind she didn't want to accept.

"I know he's family, and he's been very good to us, but why would he want to do a fool thing that could bring attention to our production plant?"

"Seems he made out very well at Belmont Park," Pete answered. "Maybe too well to have the money lying around the house."

"Whatever do you mean?" Kitty said, though she had a hunch she knew the answer. She hadn't seen her son-in-law since he rolled in from Queens late last night. The door to the bedroom he shared with Lil remained firmly closed this Sunday morning.

The day before, on October 20, 1923, racing enthusiasts at Belmont Park witnessed one of the more dramatic upsets in racing history. In racing, and betting, history it had been a memorable day for Jim. Buddy Keegan, Shamrock Stables owner, had invited him to join Harry Sinclair, the Kansas oil man who owned the Kungsholm property in the Oranges, to share his parterre-level suite at the Belmont track.

A fellow racing enthusiast, Harry owned Rancocas Stable in Jobstown. His three-year-old colt, Zev, named for his attorney, had won the Kentucky Derby and the Belmont Stakes earlier that year. Now Harry was campaigning Zev in a match race against Papyrus, the English champion proclaimed by many as the greatest horse in the world. But Jim knew better. As Buddy would later recount, the Shepherd never lacked an opinion when it came to horses and races, and made many healthy scores backing the kind of opinions that launch the career of a successful bookmaker. That day Jim made the rounds of Belmont's bookmakers, getting down as much action as he could get on Zev at odds of 5-to-1, and higher for himself, Buddy, Harry, and a few close friends who also showed up in the suite to catch the special match.

With an unprecedented $100,000 purse on the line, and 50,000 people in the stands, Zev splashed through the mud to score an astounding upset with Hall of Fame jockey Earl Sande, the original Yankee Doodle Dandy, in the irons. The result? Jim and company had pocketed some serious coin.

When Jim arrived home, he woke up his wife by showering her with a rain of paper money.

"I was king of the wise guys!" said Lil's jubilant husband.

From down the hall, Kitty had heard her daughter cry out, "Oh, sweet Jesus!"

With Kitty's begrudging blessing and Jim's new bankroll, when Monday came, Frank, Pete, Jim, and Bill Grabowski, whom the Dodd brothers decided to hire away from the Essex County Country Club, went on a shopping expedition. Hirsh Solomon, Murph's father, had brokered an introduction to Eddy Dwyer, one of his accounting clients in Newark.

Up on North Broad Street, Eddy had built a paint and wallpaper store. In reality it was a false front for his speakeasy. Known only to Newark's inner circle, Eddy had named his operation The Zoba Room. As an extra precaution, he hired bouncers as the store's staff to run the retail business during the day and into the early evening hours to keep up appearances and filter out any Treasury agents or law-abiding policemen. The room's last patron had to be in before 9 p.m. when the store officially closed for the night. Regulars could stay until the liquor ran out; the rear exit was through the attached 19th century carriage house, a throwback to the previous century when this end of North Broad had been residential.

"I think Ma forgets we've inherited our business smarts from her," Pete confided in his brother.

"Well, we'll just have to prove ourselves," Frank responded. "We can be as liberated as the women when it comes to running a covert operation."

After New Jersey ratified the Volstead Act, Newark's 1,400 bars and restaurants struggled to stay open without product to sell. Eddy and Hirsh bought a lot of decommissioned bar and kitchen equipment, and stored their merchandise in the garage. The old-fashioned carriage bays were crammed to the rafters with an enormous assortment of chrome and wooden bars, fancy carved and mirrored barbacks, dining booths, coolers and iceboxes, kitchen ranges, tables for two and four, chairs and stools, geometrically shaped mirrors, Oriental rugs, glassware, china, and one row of extravagantly potted faux palms in black and white ceramic cache pots.

Frank was fascinated.

"Where did you get the palms?"

"The Robert Treat Hotel," Eddy said. "Management over-invested in this new style designers call Art Deco."

Pete, Jim, and Bill were looking at the mahogany bars outfitted with brass rails and a set of old-fashioned spittoons.

"A new era is dawning, boys," Frank informed them, tagging all the Deco pieces he could find, including the fake palm trees. "We're going modern."

Frank also spied a sixty-six-key upright, gleaming in black lacquer, and negotiated to add the piano to the growing inventory.

"And we'll also take the tea cups and saucers for our lady guests," he said. "A couple of gallons of orchid paint, and The Place is in business."

Several weeks after the DiNicholangelo-Leinhart's annual *Columberfest* Parade on Liberty Street, Kitty heard a series of hard raps at the front door. The Dodds, the Ryans and Bobby Browne, who was still sleeping on the living room sofa, had just sat down to dinner.

"Oh, look who's here," boomed Pete, who, as a precaution, had become the family's unofficial doorman. "It's our very own Officer Blessington, coming to grace us with his presence in his nice new blue uniform. Are you here to have more than dessert this time?"

"Don't mind if I do, if I'm invited to," Pat grinned at his own silly rhyme which prompted a giggle from Doris.

"Why, sure, come in Pat," said Kitty. "We'll just set up a chair from the kitchen."

Kitty was serving a lamb roast. Frank was carving. Lil poured from a pitcher. Pat found his place between Kitty and Doris.

"I tell you, it's quite an interesting job, working for the O.P.D.," Pat began. "Let me tell you about your one and only neighbor who lives over on Day Street."

Pat winked at Doris. "He lives over a store. It gives him a nice view."

Doris obligingly giggled again.

"The man's name is Danny Sesoree. Ever hear of him?"

Everyone shook their heads.

"He's a real gadfly, Danny is. He attends the City Council meetings to complain that public works has it in for him. He recently griped that the new garbage can he paid one dollar for is being dented on purpose to get back at him for speaking his mind at meetings. Can you imagine that?"

Pat turned to Doris, who nodded solemnly.

"Then one night Car 53 was parked over on North Center Street, and Danny spied it out his back window. So he went down to check it out. Claims to have caught the officer napping while on duty.

"He went back to his apartment, phoned the department and demanded we send another patrol car out to wake him up. Sergeant Sharkey didn't call him back. So at the next council meeting Danny gets up to complain about West Orange's finest sleeping on the job."

"'Did you investigate my complaint?'"

"'Yes, we did Mr. Sesoree', said Mayor Reilly."

"'Well?'"

"'We learned Officer McGurk wasn't sleeping, Mr. Sesoree.'"

"'I saw him twice! I looked in the car and he didn't move!'"

"'No,no, no, we're not saying you're wrong.'"

"'Well, what happened?'"

"'He had died two hours before of a massive heart attack.'"

Stunned and confusion, Danny Sesoree finally stammered, "'Oh, I'm so sorry. I understand. My mistake. Even I can make a mistake.'"

Pat's story drew chuckles from everyone.

"Then two days ago, just as Sergeant Sharkey was coming on for desk duty, another call came in from Danny," said Pat, resuming his Sesoree saga.

"He's been observing all kinds of activity going on between the public works yard and that new company on North Center Street, Acme Chemical.

"Now, while Danny *is* pleased to see the abandoned property put to good use, well, when he saw a sanitation truck dumping crushed stone in Acme's parking lot, followed by a bulldozer leveling it off, he didn't think was right.

"So he phoned the P.D. Got Sergeant Sharkey, and explained what he had observed."

"'I will get right back to you, Mr. Sesoree.'"

"Five minutes later he phoned Danny back."

"'Mr. Sesoree, I just talked to the mayor's office and learned they have a new policy for something called public-private participation. The city will receive free chemical supplies in exchange for excess material the city has laying around.'"

"'What a wonderful arrangement!' Mr. Sesoree cried enthusiastically. 'The city government is saving us taxpayers money! Oh, thank you for the return phone call, Officer Sharkey.'"

Laughter rippled around the table, and Pat Blessington nodded, more with encouragement than approval.

"I'm glad I've got you feeling good about how the force is looking out for you," he said, "because I'm also here to give you a word of warning. Sergeant Sharkey told me I was hired because they had to fire Jock Sanders for beating up some of the store owners on Main Street."

A collective gasp from Kitty, Lil, and even Doris rose up.

"Not John Monteverdi?" asked Kitty.

"No, not John. Sanders was smart enough not to take on any Italian shopkeepers. Knew there could be serious repercussions. But it's clear he was trying to muscle hush money for all the illegal liquor that's getting distributed around the Oranges," Pat explained. "The chief fired him."

"Thank God," Lil said. "That low-lying good-for-nothing…" She looked at Doris and then at her husband.

"He's gone over to Treasury in Newark," Pat continued. "Claims he's gone legit. Says he's going to bring down every illegal immigrant caught with hooch. He tells everyone he meets he's got a real badge that's backed by the Feds.

"I thought you should know."

Al Leinhart at work in Edison's factory. Uncle Jim.

Pete, at left, is about to KO his competitor
on board the *USS George Washington.*

Frank and the second-hand Model T Ford that went to County Cork…

…in exchange for this snazzy Packard LeBaron!

When Irish eyes are smiling: Frank, Lil and Pete.

The lovely Leinhart sisters: Clara, Dolly, Loretta (who married Elton Tierney), Marie (the author's mother), and Dot.

Ready for Repeal: Frank smiles for the camera
as The Place becomes Dodd's Tavern.

Frank, Buster and Pete sampling the product!

Chapter 5: Doris, Drake, and Dutch

Doris Ryan and Clara Leinhart were best of friends. During Liberty Street's annual spring and fall musicales, they made quite the comical pair as they marched side-by-side: Doris, delicately holding her shiny triangle and Clara, waving the heavily padded mallets of the family's glockenspiel, occasionally hitting the right notes as her sisters pushed the ungainly instrument along.

Now on the verge of graduating from Orange High School, they were becoming young women in an age when hemlines were high and waistlines were low. The roomy dresses worn by flappers could be made to swish seductively, allowing for the occasional glimpse of a knee. Most dramatic was what the girls had done to their long tresses. While Kitty wore her thick white hair in a traditional bun and both girls' mothers had shoulder-length hair swept in a Gibson girl up-do, the teenagers sported bobs. Doris, whose coal-black hair inherited the curl of the Ryan side of the family, had a Marcel wave, her hair falling in a series of soft waves that nicely framed her face.

Clara had the classic Dutch bob with bangs and a blunt cut.

Doris had grown up noticeably different from the Ryans or Dodds. A mandatory junior-year poise class heightened Doris's awareness that there was another way to live life than what her extended family was experiencing. She took to correcting her father and even her beloved Uncle Frank about using the proper fork at meal times. The upper-class young ladies in her high school made it painfully obvious that their fathers earned livings in respectable professions; several were bank presidents and a number of them commuted to high-level positions in New York City.

"I love my family," Doris often thought, "and I'd die for my grandmother, even if she is a bootlegger. My father is a bookie and my uncles run an illegal bar. Why couldn't my family have been in legitimate businesses that I could talk about? Was I switched at birth?"

It was late spring in 1928, a Sunday night, and Doris and Clara had permission for a sleep-over; the two would go to school together from Kitty's home. Doris still had the back bedroom overlooking smelly Edison Brook, a fact that added to her discomfort over how her family made its money. A year after John Dodd's death, Kitty had given up the front master bedroom to Lil and Jim. Frank and Pete moved into the couple's old room, which was slightly larger than their own, and Kitty took the brothers' former bedroom next to Doris's.

Though the lights were off, the teenagers were not asleep. Still to be thoroughly discussed was a strategy for lobbying their mothers to let them to wear make-up. Suddenly, shots rang from outside the house. Then, a volley from within the Dodd home responded. The fusillade coming from her parents' bedroom surprised Doris. When had her father purchased a gun? Downstairs, her uncles had been playing cards. Had they suspected something was going to happen tonight?

In the eerily still aftermath, Kitty tapped on Doris's door.

"Are you girls alright in there?"

"Yes, Grandma," Doris said. "Are you?"

"Yes, child. There's nothing to worry about," Kitty added, sending up a silent prayer of gratitude to Saint Anne. "This will all be taken care of."

As Kitty returned to her own bed, she wondered just who had had been out there. Frank, Pete, and even Jim, had been prepared. But for whom? A Treasury agent? A rogue cop from the Oranges? Or, did the Dodds have an unknown enemy within the tightly-knit group of Liberty Street families?

Later Monday morning Frank put in a call to Buster Gilmore, the Oranges' Animal Control Officer.

"We had an attempted break-in last night," Frank explained to his long-time friend from their days at McGee's Gym. "We need a police dog. The bigger, the better. Do you have any dogs like that at the pound?"

"No, we don't have any shepherds or any big dogs right now," said Buster. "Give me a couple of days to see what I can do."

Buster and his family were part of the Oranges' East Ward, the long-established African-American community that had helped elect Russell Reilly to office. The family matriarch was Mrs. Gilmore, a midwife whose husband was a successful dry cleaner. Both were active in the Bethel Baptist Church. Among their three children, two were outstanding athletes at Orange High. Alice, the only daughter, was six-foot-one, and excelled at track and field. Robby trained at McGee's Gym. But Buster, at six-foot-five and the most muscular of the three, was a paradox. He had no interest in sports, was the best-dressed, and was the most well-spoken of the Gilmore siblings. Mrs. Gilmore wondered more than once whether he, like

Doris Ryan, had been switched at birth.

After Russ Reilly's mayoral win, Buster agreed to run the dog pound on North Center Street. But he had two conditions. First, he wanted a motorized truck to replace the department's outdated horse and wagon. Second, he wanted the title of Animal Control Officer. Mayor Reilly gladly met both.

After hanging up the phone, Buster turned to the bulletin board by his desk and looked at a clipping from the Sunday edition of the *Newark News* pinned there earlier that morning. The article featured a picture of Sergeant York, the most famous World War I military dog ever to be decorated. For two years he ran messages through the trench lines. Twice the shepherd had been wounded. The photo showed a fearsome black-and-tan dog, larger than average, with a noticeably vivid scar across one eyebrow. Part of his tail was missing. He was the kind of dog that didn't encourage human contact. The *News* reported that Newark was in the running to buy Sergeant York. It intended to start a canine core in a joint effort with the U.S. Treasury Department to combat bootlegging in Newark.

Buster called the 67th Street National Guard Armory in Manhattan, which was arranging for Sergeant York's transfer, and identified himself as Newark's dog warden, Tom Brown. Buster told the officer who answered the phone that he'd be in the next day to pick up the shepherd. Then followed a series of phone calls to put his plan in motion. He called Danny Paris next.

"I need two business cards for a special project for Frank Dodd," he said. "One has to read Deputy Mayor of Newark, Meyer Ellenstein. The other has to read Tom Brown, Dog Warden. Both have to have the city seal on it. I'm also going to need the seal and the words 'Newark Dog Pound' on signs for my truck."

Next Buster called Harold 'Swing Time' Riker, the loquacious supervisor of the Oranges Public Works Department and asked him to take the next day off duty, but to wear a suit and tie and be at the animal control office at 9 a.m.

"I'm going to need you for a special pick-up," he said to the always accommodating Swing Time. "Thing is, you can't be too chatty when we get there."

Buster's final call went to Irving Overby, a photographer with a budding business in the East Ward.

"Bring your camera gear," he directed, "and wear the good threads you use for weddings."

On Tuesday the trio powered the motorized truck over the Pulaski Skyway, through Jersey City, into the Holland Tunnel, and up to the 67th Street Armory. Once there, they presented the business cards made by Danny while Irving snapped pictures. The commanding officer was quite impressed that Newark had sent its deputy mayor and a photographer to record the event.

"Good to meet you Deputy Mayor Ellenstein," he said, vigorously pumping Swing Time's right arm and moving his body to stand next to him for the first photo op. "We're honored the great city of Newark won the bid on getting the most decorated dog in military history."

In fact, the officer wasn't the least bit shy about posing in every photograph with, and without, Sergeant York who seemed to cast a look of disdain at all the civilian hoopla. Finally, Buster gingerly loaded the big dog into the truck, telling the officer that the fee would be wired that afternoon. With a friendly wave, the three men and Sergeant York headed to the Oranges.

"Why, Buster, what a fine-looking canine," Kitty cautiously said, a little while later. She took a careful step backwards as the ferocious-looking Sergeant York made it up the steps. She took a second step of retreat as the military canine took command of her kitchen. "I can't wait to hear what Peggy McNichols might say about him."

Summer's all-too-brief interlude was fast approaching Labor Day. Doris had graduated Orange High with distinction, but chose to spend the ensuing months working in the family business and enjoying the now customary Fourth of July vacation in Manasquan. This last August weekend she was helping her grandmother do chores on Liberty Street when Kitty indicated it was time for tea.

"September is coming up, child," Kitty said, turning the water on to boil as Doris set out the Lenox cups and saucers. "What would you like to do next with your life?"

"Grandma, I'm making more money working at Acme Chemical than the girls in my Orange graduating class."

"No, dear, think beyond Acme. This will end someday. Either, we will get caught," Kitty paused to shudder slightly, "or the government will come to its senses and repeal this damn prohibition law."

"Well," Doris drawled, searching for an answer to satisfy her grandmother. "I don't know. Do we have enough money for me to go to school?"

Kitty got up from the kitchen table and went to the counter where she opened a drawer and pulled out an advertisement from the *Newark News.* It read:

Drake Academy for Progressive Young Women
We train our graduates in two years
for management or
to own their own businesses
Faculty and guest lecturers come from esteemed positions
Since 1883

Doris eyes lit up. "Grandma, can I do this?"

"Yes," Kitty replied. "The family has made money enough to cover all the tuition and all the costs, plus some new clothes. Let's go down and sign you up."

When Tuesday morning came, Kitty and Doris took the trolley to Main Street and stepped off at Mura's Department Store. The Drake Academy stood directly across the street, in an imposing four-story building chiseled from granite. Grandmother and granddaughter linked arms, crossed Main, and climbed the steps.

Once inside they approached the receptionist's desk. The plaque read: Geraldine Durr.

"May I help you?"

"I'd like to enroll my granddaughter in Drake Academy," Kitty began.

"I'm sorry, but today is orientation for all those who registered in August," Miss Durr said.

Just then, a tall, strikingly good-looking blonde-haired woman who moved with the swift grace of an athlete crossed the hall behind the reception desk and overheard the exchange. Taking in the tableaux of a well-dressed matron who radiated success and means, and a stylishly dressed young lady in a cloche hat, she presumed to be either a niece or granddaughter, she spoke up.

"Why don't you come to my office? I'm the director, Lisbeth Reich. Come this way."

Miss Reich led the pair into a mahogany-paneled room that overlooked the bustling Main Street. After everyone was seated, and introductions were made, Miss Reich opened the conversation.

"As you might be aware, here at Drake, we are in the business of thoroughly preparing young women to be leaders in their communities," she said. "Our graduates go to work in banks, in stock brokerages, and even onto the factory floors."

"Yes," Kitty, nodded, impressed with the director's forthright manner.

"We also teach family planning according to the method espoused by Margaret Sanger," Miss Reich continued, "so young women can be properly ready to have children when they want them."

Kitty and Doris nodded.

"We ask for a serious commitment of two years," she said, "at the end of which we promise a very good placement. After all, we have quite an alumnae pool since our first graduating class in 1883."

"But I am too late to get in this year?" Doris asked, now worried that she had waited too long to think about the future that could be hers if she were to graduate from Drake. Secretly, Kitty was pleased her granddaughter had spoken up. It had been right to show her the advertisement.

"We do have a few places left in the Class of 1930," Miss Reich said, "that's why we ran the advertisement in the *Newark News*. We prefer to run at full enrollment. Would you like me to ask Miss Durr to bring in the paperwork? If you are prepared to pay today, we could introduce Doris at the start of the 11 a.m. session in which incoming students meet the professors?"

Kitty nodded, opening her purse and proceeding to extract a series of $100 bills. Miss Reich appeared unfazed, instead pressing a buzzer on the inside of her desk that summoned Geraldine to bring the enrollment forms.

Thrilled at this turn of events in her life and the possibilities the future held, Doris leaned from under her hat brim to kiss her grandmother.

"Thank you, Grandma," she said.

Still counting out the tuition money, Kitty barely paused to remind her granddaughter, "Thank your parents when they come home from their second honeymoon in Manasquan."

Several months went by as Doris happily adjusted to the progressive curriculum at Drake Academy. She was on campus eight hours a day, five days a week. Doris especially loved the social freedom she found in occasionally staying late in the Oranges' downtown to have dinner with her new-found friends who came from well-to-do and well-established families.

One day, shortly before Easter in the spring semester of 1929, Miss Reich invited Doris into her office.

"I hear good reports about your progress at Drake," she said. "How do you like your courses?"

Doris smiled and told the director she was so appreciative to be in this particular class of young women.

Miss Reich let a moment of silence pass. Smiling encouragingly at Doris, she said, "We know your family is involved in the distribution business." Another pause. "I know it's the liquor industry. And there's nothing whatsoever wrong about it because I believe they are simply anticipating the repeal of this stupid prohibition law, especially as evidence mounts that federal agents aren't doing an effective job."

Inwardly, Doris was mortified. Just that very morning she had had an exchange with her grandmother about Al Capone. Kitty had kept a headline about the St. Valentine's Day Massacre in Chicago taped to their new refrigerator.

"Grandma, Al Capone is a gangster. He kills people. I bet he eats babies for breakfast."

"Oh, Doris, people say terrible things when you're on top and successful," Kitty had responded. "Here is a man who said 'I simply give people what they want.' Why, we're doing the same thing."

Doris brought her attention back to Miss Reich.

"As you know by now, we invite the fathers of our students to come in as guest lecturers," she was saying. "We here at the Drake Academy believe there is a beneficial opportunity to inform our students about how to comport themselves in various business venues. Many women can now enter a speakeasy and drink with the kind of ease they were denied in bars prior to the Federal Prohibition Amendment. At the same time, the reality is that so much business is done in a social settings involving alcohol."

Miss Reich paused again to let Doris absorb this information.

"We'd like your father to be our guest speaker for April and lecture on how women should correctly behave in this particular setting."

Doris smiled meekly. How could she refuse Miss Reich who had so graciously accepted her into the Drake Academy program? Moreover, Doris couldn't fathom quitting because her experience at Drake had come to mean so much to her. But how was she going to bridge her new world of socially connected friends with her family's world of secrecy?

Later that evening, to Doris's shocked surprise, her father agreed to the proposal.

"I would be honored," he said. "I'm not much of a public speaker, but I hope to do you proud."

Almost 200 students, faculty and staff filled Drake's auditorium the day of Jim's special lecture. Kitty, Lil, and Doris were invited to sit in the front row alongside the director.

Jim stepped up to the microphone.

"Thank you, Miss Reich, for inviting me to speak here today on this important topic. It is still a new experience to see women in bars. Despite federal amendments, they aren't going away, either.

"So here is a simple rule for keeping your own counsel. Stay focused on your purpose. If you are there to dance, only have one drink. If you are there to hear the music, only have one drink. If you are there for business or to meet your boyfriend, or possibly your future husband, only have just one drink. If you are there to meet your friends and have a good time, you can have more than one drink, but make that only two drinks you have all night long."

Jim paused to survey the crowded assembly hall.

"Men will try to get you drunk. That's not new to Prohibition. If a man becomes obnoxious, hit him in the solar plexus with the heel of your hand," Jim paused to show where on his chest to find the solar plexus. "When you hit a man there, it will take his breath away, no matter how tall or short you are.

"After you've struck him, take him by the elbow and lead him to the door. If you are feeling hospitable, you could ask, 'Do you feel better now?'"

Like light rippling across the water, the sound of female laughter greeted Jim's suggestion of a solicitous question to a crippled attacker.

For forty minutes Jim talked before his unrehearsed speech took an unexpected turn.

"It's been difficult for my family, having an alcoholic affect the lives of my wife, my mother-in-law, and her two sons who are my business partners. But no one has suffered more than my daughter whom I love with all my heart. She has always been the youngest member of our family and was cheated of her grandfather's love and attention and of ours while we tried to take care of him."

Sitting between her mother and grandmother, Doris could feel tears slowly falling down her cheeks. She had never heard her father talk about the Dodd family in this intimate a manner, and so publicly. Quickly she stole a glance at the women on the women on either side of her and saw tears well up in the eyes of Lil and Kitty.

"I want to apologize for all that my daughter has had to go through. I love her more than life itself," Jim said again for emphasis.

Acknowledging Miss Reich, he added, "This is the greatest privilege to be asked to speak before the Drake Academy. Thank you."

Dabbing her eyes, Miss Reich got up from her seat.

"Mr. Ryan," she said, as she got to the podium and reached in to extract a framed certificate. "The Drake Academy for Progressive Young Women wishes to thank you for your invaluable advice, insight, and perspicacity today and confer upon you the honorary title of professor of commerce. Will you accept?"

Surprised and speechless, Jim could only nod. The audience burst into a sustained round of applause. Doris jumped out of her chair to lead a standing ovation. As Miss Reich shook his hand, Jim leaned in and said, "If you would like to have a special night at The Place to help your students become familiar with this kind of business setting, you just give me the word and we will close it down for a private party."

Miss Reich was extremely pleased with Jim's spontaneous offer, and nodded as the clapping continued unabated.

"We'll contact the parents and get permission forms and ask some of the faculty and staff to come along as chaperones," she whispered back.

"Why don't we plan it as a Tax Day Party? As your new professor of commerce, I have it on good authority that the accountants and politicians are negotiating for April 15 as a permanent answer to the 16th Amendment."

Miss Reich nodded again, her smile broadening into a grin. Her latest guest speaker was offering more than just a bonus with his party offer at The Place: he was giving her female students a competitive advantage in finding jobs and summer internships with this news about a uniform tax-filing day.

Jim, together with Frank, Pete and Bill Grabowski, set about spiffing up The Place for the Drake women's coming-out party Monday night, ordering vases of pink roses to go with the black-white-and-lavender decor. Frank put out the porcelain cups and saucers he'd bought from Eddy Dwyer. Each table carried a miniature candle *torchiere* shaped like a lily. To impress the progressive young women from the Drake Academy, Danny Paris designed cocktail napkins embroidered with the initials D.A.P.Y.W.

Creating a guest list from the RSVPs forwarded by Miss Reich, the men hired the up-and-coming boxer 'Two-Ton' Tony Galento to keep out the undesirables. Fortunately for all, he was available. The following night, however, he was scheduled to fight George Neron at McGee's Gym.

Everyone from the Rue de Liberté Philharmonic Marching Orchestra was invited to perform, particularly the sisters, Stash, from the Jablonski family. Elton Tierney was put on notice to attend, wearing his Scottish kilt. For good measure, Frank hired menswear model and aspiring actor Fred Weber to tickle the ivories. With his matinee-idol looks and fancy footwork on the dance floor, Fred would be a hit with the Drake ladies.

Where Frank stood from his vantage point in the middle of the oval-shaped bar, he could watch the party-goers filtering in. The faculty members were easy to identify. A dowdy-looking bunch; *old school, Frank said to himself.* The young Drake women flounced in wearing colorful tube dresses and beaded headbands accented with elegant feathers; *that's more like it, he thought.* As the flurry of arrivals swelled, a statuesque platinum blonde in a low-waisted coral dress with a kerchief hem and black patent leather pumps emerged.

Frank immediately took notice; *those long legs are worth a turn on the dance floor. I wonder who she is.*

Frank didn't have to wait long to find out. The *doll* was none other than Miss Reich, the Drake Academy's director, said Jim when he made the introductions. When the time came to pour his niece her first cup of whiskey, Frank made a big show of it. Doris was counting on a song, and she was not disappointed. Neither was Miss Reich for whom the song was intended. Out of his repertoire, Frank pulled a popular tune penned four years earlier in Atlantic City, and in his trademark Irish tenor, crooned to a hushed crowd:

I'm discontented with homes that I've rented
So I have invented my own.
Darling, this place is lovely oasis
Where life's weary taste is unknown
Far from the crowded city
Where flowers pretty caress the stream
Cozy to hide in, to live side by side in,
Don't let it apart in my dream-

Picture you upon my knee
Just tea for two
And two for tea
Me for you
And you for me…

As femininely sophisticated as The Place looked Monday night, by Saturday Frank and Pete had transformed their speakeasy's interior back into its Art Deco origins in preparation for the retirement party being thrown for the Oranges' police captain, Edward Donahue. The entire force was expected, along with city officials, department heads, and assorted representatives from the Liberty Street families. At Acme Chemical, it had been a long week, so Kitty decided to stay home. With Jim squiring his wife out on a dinner date in Newark, Doris opted to keep her beloved grandmother company in case Sergeant York needed a back up.

Once again Frank reached out to the Jablonski twins to help provide the entertainment for the evening. They obliged his request, happy to perform on their accordions Mummer show tunes they recently learned in Philadelphia. Frank also brought back Fred Weber to play Irish drinking songs at the piano so the sisters could have an occasional break and mingle with the hometown crowd. Lobster Lil's sent over platters of freshly cooked seafood and iced clams. John Monteverdi supplied corned beef while Jimmy Jimmy brought in sauerkraut and boiled potatoes he cured himself. The spread was enough to feed two retirement parties.

Everyone was having a good time when two thickly built muscle men shouldered their way to the bar and beckoned Frank over. From the bar's far end, Pete took notice and joined his brother. He remembered the two from last week. In distinct Teutonic accents, with no attempt at pleasantries, they had flatly told the brothers they wanted 'in' on the Dodd operation.

Pete and Frank had laughed them off, telling the two ~ *What did you say your names were? Fritz and Hans?* ~ there was no Dodd operation.

"We don't know what you're talking about," Frank had said, bending slightly to pull a baseball bat from under the counter.

Now Fritz and Hans had returned, flashing a bankroll of $100 bills Pete estimated at $2,000. But more seriously than the cash were the pair of .38 pistols the two Germans ever so slightly revealed as they leaned up against the bar.

Quickly, Frank put up a couple of highball glasses and poured gin into them, indicating the drinks were on the house.

"How did a couple of guys just off the boat get that kind of cash?" Pete whispered to his brother.

Frank shook his head. "Did you notice the guns?"

Pete nodded. "This wasn't the night to leave ours at home."

As the evening wore on, Frank kept the Germans' glasses continually filled in hopes of discouraging anymore questions about Acme Chemical. Just as he was thinking about going to Buster Gilmore for help, one of the Jablonski sisters let out a piercing yelp as Hans grabbed hold of her caboose. She wheeled around and landed a vicious slap across his face. Momentarily stunned, but still standing, Hans roughly pushed her away from him and into the crowd. She stumbled. The commotion brought Fritz over. As the two men opened their jackets and went for their .38s, out of nowhere 15 guns were drawn and aimed right at their heads. In one synchronous click, all the gun holders pulled back their hammers.

In the brief moment of silence that followed, Pat Blessington moved in and quickly removed the .38s. Then all at once, the cops, who had been enjoying Ed Donahue's send-off, started fighting over who'd get to cuff the interlopers and charge them with disturbing their revelry. A squad car arrived and the pair was whisked away to police headquarters. Fritz and Hans were booked, finger-printed, had their mug shots taken, and were given a receipt for the $2,000 cash. Then they were unceremoniously thrown into the drunk tank.

In what seemed a few short hours later that Sunday morning, a guard woke them up, giving them a minimum breakfast of a donut and coffee along with standard-issue razors and shaving cream.

"What these for?" Fritz asked through a groggy haze.

"Your hearing's in one hour."

"Hearing?" asked Hans, tentatively holding his head in his hands, not knowing if he wanted to puke or die.

"In Prohibition Court. You've committed some serious crimes. You're charged with attempted murder, disrupting the peace, attempted robbery..."

Fritz interrupted, "We were at blind pig!"

"There are no blind pigs in the Oranges."

"What hell is this?"

"This is Pleasant Valley where there is no hell for those who abide by the law."

The police had a way of dealing with wealthy citizens whose self-righteous indignation grated every public servant and common citizen. They'd set up a Sunday morning mock trial, fine the social miscreant, and divide the levy among the civic actors.

The court room was located on the second floor of City Hall. That morning's judge was a young Seton Hall University law student by the name of Mickey Brown. Regarded as a genius, the 21-year-old was in his last year of law school. To compensate for his boyish demeanor which frequently caused people to think he was 19, Mickey kept his hair closely cropped. A judge's black robes heightened his efforts at being taken seriously.

Based on an early morning phone call, Jim Ryan brought Doris who had a new Kodak Brownie camera with a flash bulb attachment. She wore her father's fedora with a press card stuck in the hatband. Courtesy of Danny Paris, the card read *Newark News*.

As Jim and Doris made their way across the plaza to the City Hall steps they ran into John and Mary Monteverdi who had just left mid-morning mass at St. John's Church. The couple made a handsome pair; he in a dapper brand-new felt hat and Chesterfield overcoat, she in a very fashionable spring dress, wrapped in a mink stole to ward of the morning chill. They were on the way to their grocery store to check inventory when Jim stopped them.

"John, Mary, could you spare us a half hour? There's a little problem up at City Hall, and we'd appreciate it if you could help us out."

"Yes, yes, we'd be glad to help. What is it?" John replied.

"It's a special court hearing. I think you'll get a kick out of it," Jim added, leading them inside and up to the second floor.

"Ah, Mrs. Monteverdi," said Judge Mickey Brown, the mock court's theatrical director. "I'm glad to meet you finally. Thank you for volunteering your time to help us this morning.

"You are the new court clerk. Here is a pad and pen."

"But I don't..."

"Just sit here right in front of the bench and write whatever you want," Mickey directed. "Mr. Monteverdi, if you will sit with Mr. Ryan."

Just then Jimmy Polmeri, one of Mickey's classmates, walked in to take up the role of prosecuting attorney. Behind him came the court-appointed attorney for the two Germans, Buster Gilmore.

A small phalanx of police officers marched in the two defendants. Behind them filed other officers, some in uniforms for the day's shift and others still in their clothes from Ed Donahue's party.

Fred Weber read off the charges: attempted murder, attempted robbery, causing a riot, disrupting the peace.

Hans jumped up. "I never heard anything like this."

Mickey sternly looked down from the bench in his black robe, banged the gavel. "One more outburst like that and you're going back to jail without a hearing."

Buster jumped up. "I object your honor, I object."

"What do you object to?"

"I object to everything."

Fritz and Hans sat there dumbfounded and not a little hung

over. A little less than a month ago they were in Gelsenkirchen. Shortly after landing in Newark, they made contact with the city's underworld of unemployed beer brewers. Then, forty-eight hours ago mobster Longy Zwillman gave them each a $1,000 to buy that "hooch from the Oranges made by those Dodds."

Now they were in court with a giant of a black man as their lawyer.

Mickey called a side bar for both attorneys. Once at the bench, the three men began discussing the upcoming horse season at Belmont Park.

From the press box, Doris stood up and requested permission of Judge Brown to take pictures of the accused for the Monday morning edition of the *Newark News*.

Buster turned around and asked his clients, "Do you want your picture in tomorrow's paper? No?"

Buster walked over to the defendants' table.

"Then maybe it's time to talk about a settlement. If you each plead guilty, you will get off with a fine and maybe no jail time."

"But we were in a pig," Fritz protested. "Guns everywhere."

"There are no speakeasies in the Oranges," Buster replied, leaning into his clients. "You should know that by now."

Judge Brown called another side bar. Mickey, Buster and Jimmy Polmeri talked about the weather. Before too long, Mickey broke off the discussion.

"The bench wishes to recognize the Honorable Russell Reilly, our city's great crime-fighting mayor. He heard about this terrible incident and is here in attendance. Would you please rise?"

Everybody looked around, craning their necks to get a look at the mayor. Suddenly Jim Ryan poked John Monteverdi in the ribs.

"That's you."

John stood up and took a bow. It was all Mary Monteverdi could do to not burst out laughing.

In the end, Fritz and Hans paid the fine: $1,990 out of the $2,000 they brought with them from Newark. A police escort led them to the No. 21 trolley and waited until the pair was firmly on board before returning to duty. Back at City Hall, Mickey divided the fine money among the cast.

"This beats the hell out of going home and putting a meatloaf in the oven," agreed the Monteverdis who walked out of the municipal building, arm-in-arm, laughing.

Located around the corner from the Robert Treat Hotel, the Palace Chop House served Newark's working class. Only the cognoscenti were permitted down a narrow hall to a rear dining room where a bar stretched between the kitchen wall and the back paneled wall that hid a door to the alley.

Under a single light bulb that cast an orange glow around the room, two men in business suits sat at a table covered in linen and set for lunch with a small brass vase filled with fake violets at its center. Two disheveled men stood before them. Two men in topcoats stood at the back wall, their arms by their sides, right hands fitted with guns.

Finally, after a long explanation in broken English, Fritz concluded with, "Dodds, they control whole Oranges."

Beside him, Hans blinked several times.

Longie Zwillman, king of Newark's illegal beer trade, and his New York counterpart, Dutch Schultz, shook their heads.

"You were sent there to bring back product. You were given $2,000. And the cops arrest you on charges of disturbing the peace?!" Zwillman was still incredulous.

"Who are these Dodds?" Schultz asked.

Fritz and Hans remained silent.

"They're running whiskey and gin in the Watchung Mountains," Zwillman answered. "I heard a story that the real brains behind the operation is an old lady with a white bun who wears black. You see anyone like that there?"

Again, Fritz and Hans said nothing.

"Worthless," Schultz spit out.

"Get 'em out of here," Zwillman said, cocking his head to the two body guards at the back door.

"A dame, huh?" Schultz said after the four men disappeared into the alley.

Zwillman shrugged. "All kinds of crazy things have gone on ever since they got the right to vote."

He got up from the table and walked over to the bar where there was a telephone and dialed a number.

"Hirsh," he barked into the phone. "What can you do to get me the head of the operation over there in the Oranges? Yeah, you know which one I mean. And if you don't, ask your son. Doesn't he still work for Edison?"

A little while later on Liberty Street, Jim Ryan carefully hung up the phone in the living room. Doris hadn't come home yet from the academy. Lil was finishing the bookkeeping at Acme Chemical, and Jim could count on Al Leinhart and Elton Tierney to walk her safely home.

Frank and Pete were finishing their dinner before leaving to open The Place. Kitty sat crocheting on the new sofa the family bought after Bobby Browne found his own apartment. When he finally moved out, the family gave him the old couch as a housewarming gift.

"Kitty," Jim began, "I've got something I need to talk over with you and the boys."

Kitty looked up from her needlework, her face a mask in

response to her son-in-law's cautious tone. Her father's words from long ago rushed from her childhood memory to connect with her present: *Don't smile.*

As Jim laid out the details of Hirsh Solomon's phone call, Frank and Pete listened in a stunned silence. There was a long pause before anyone in the living room spoke.

"It's business," Kitty said, matter-of-factly. *Don't frown.* "I'll go down tomorrow."

There was a quick intake of breath as Frank and Pete both sucked air in through their teeth.

"On the trolley," she added. *Don't look over your shoulder.* "Not a word to Doris or to Lil."

Kitty's tone left no margin for protest.

The next morning, Jim walked his mother-in-law to the trolley stop on Main Street

"I would come with you," he said.

"No, Jim, someone needs to stay here and shepherd the family's business." Kitty's voice was firm, but not unkind. She knotted a dark green chiffon scarf around her neck and tucked the ends into her black cloth coat.

At 11 a.m. Kitty arrived at the Palace Chop House and made her way inside. Once her eyes adjusted to the gloom, she noticed a waiter walking over to her.

If you come upon them in the road, always look straight ahead.

"Mrs. Dodd, this way." He pointed to the hallway. Kitty walked into the rear dining room, noting that its linen-draped tables and mirrored bar back put it cut above the plain front room where the public ate.

"Won't you have a seat, Mrs. Dodd." Longie Zwillman proffered her a chair, the stone in his pinkie ring still managing to glint in the dim light. Dutch Schultz rose slightly from his seat across the table.

Primly, Kitty sat down. She laid her modest black purse horizontally across her lap and folded her right gloved hand on top of her left which held the strap. Under her coat, she wore the black linen dress she put on for John Dodd's funeral.

Longie cleared his throat.

"We appreciate you coming to see us, Mrs. Dodd… or may I call you Kitty?"

Kitty blinked once with her eyes.

In unison, Longie and Dutch visibly nodded.

"We're sorry for any inconvenience our associates may have caused for your family," Longie added.

Don't engage.

After a moment passed, Dutch said, "We're interested in increasing our inventory."

Kitty said nothing, her memory recalling the long hours spent working with the *damnBrits* on Haulbowline Island's garrison command.

"What we mean is," Longie broke in, instantly recognizing Dutch's mistake, "we'd like to diversify what's available in Newark… perhaps offering you a trade."

"We appreciate local suppliers," Kitty replied, emphasizing the word 'local' as she thickened her brogue.

Now it was Longie and Dutch's turn to hesitate, their eyelids blinking rapidly with this unexpected reference to territory.

"Ah, Mrs. Dodd," Longie said, "we understand that your products are top of the line…indiscernible from the real McCoy..."

"And," Kitty fixed a steely maternal gaze on Longie Zwillman as she prepared to finish his sentence, "should be matched in comparable value."

Dutch Schultz snorted at the trump.

Kitty shifted slightly in the dining chair to get the two men across the table from her to refocus on the business negotiation.

"My husband died ten years ago. He left me with five children. Times are hard. Money is tight. I've had to get by with what my father taught me years ago as a child in Ireland."

Longie and Dutch leaned in rapt attention.

She continued. "I now take my inspiration from the French widow, so maybe you can understand my need to have quality as well as variety."

Again, Kitty had chosen one word to emphasize. This time it was 'variety'.

Again, Dutch snorted.

"Pretty clever for an Irish moll, Mrs. Dodd," he said, admiringly. "If you were younger, I'd take you with me to Atlantic City."

Longie jabbed his fellow gangster with his left elbow.

"And what's happening in Atlantic City?" Kitty asked innocently.

"Just a convention of distributors," Longie said, hoping to redirect the conversation.

"Longie's twin brother will be there." Dutch couldn't resist the dig. "You know, all the papers call Longie the Al Capone of New Jersey."

"Really now, do they? Well, certainly one can see a resemblance," Kitty gave Longie an appraising gaze. "And when will the convention take place?"

"Oh, we arrive on lucky 13," Dutch said without hesitation.

Longie was about to aim his left elbow at Dutch's upper arm when he thought better of it.

"We'd be happy to make a deal with you, Mrs. Dodd, for an exchange of quality product. How about we'll call you through our same intermediary when the next shipment comes in?"

Jock Sanders took off his headphones, glad to get the weight off, and nodded to the stenographer that her work was done for the day. She, too, removed her headphones. Last year, the U.S. Supreme Court had approved the practice of wiretapping for the law enforcement and government officials. Thought he was ten blocks away at the Treasury's office on Broad and West Kinney, thanks to a wire that a workman had run through a lampshade on a wall sconce, Jock was a good as hidden-in-plain-sight in the Palace Chop House.

Chapter 6: In Plain Sight

It was the last Sunday morning in April. Kitty had the Liberty Street house to herself. Frank and Pete were up and out early to take care of some unexpected maintenance at The Place. Lil, Jim, and Doris had gone to Manhattan for a visit. Her Lenox teacup filled with Black Rose tea from Monteverdi's new selection of imported delicacies, Kitty sat at her kitchen table, engrossed in Lillian McNamara's breathless account of the Queen of Resorts' upcoming Diamond Jubilee. Loaded with photos, the feature story was prominently laid out in the *Newark News'* weekly magazine for April 28. In just a few short weeks, the eyes of the world would behold a new Atlantic City:

Extravagant Boardwalk movie palace to seat 4,300!

WPG gets state-of-the-art radio studio!

Galaxy of stars from stage and screen generate pre-Broadway buzz on the Boards!

Dancers to cha-cha-cha in new ballroom for 5,000!

A hall for conventions the size of a gridiron!!!

Kitty looked closer.

The National Electric Light Association's 50th birthday celebration for the light bulb will be the municipal auditorium's first-ever convention. The honoree is the Father of Electricity, Thomas A. Edison, the man "who lit Atlantic City"!

Well, Kitty wondered out loud, what would the old man think of that?

While everyone from engineers to lobbyists were expected for the inaugural convention in June, Kitty noted wryly that Lillian McNamara's account didn't mention the other convention whose businessmen were slated to arrive May 13. Obviously, their industries were doing quite well if they were going to convene in Atlantic City, thought Kitty. Was theirs a jubilee, too?

Despite the Federal Prohibition Amendment, the liquor business was, indeed, booming. Acme Chemical enjoyed ever-increasing sales and success. Most importantly to Kitty, her company's economic growth brought a better standard of living to everyone involved in making and distributing Acme's rye and gin. And, even though the boys' bar across the street was hidden behind old construction scaffolding, the steady traffic of speakeasy patrons hadn't attracted any Treasury agents who might want to put the Dodds out of business. That, too, was a sign of success, Kitty reasoned.

True, the family hadn't invented a light bulb or a phonograph, or a movie picture studio. And as sales territories went, the Oranges was their goldfish pond, not the enormous turf of bootleg beer and numbers running that Longie Zwillman and Dutch Schultz oversaw. Yet, Acme's achievements were noteworthy.

Kitty slapped her right palm down on top of the open Sunday magazine. Why not have an Acme jubilee?! A family conference?! In Atlantic City?! A week's stay in what McNamara reported was the *World's Playground* could open new avenues of opportunity. And, Kitty decided, she'd finally get to see what it was like to live the high life among the high rollers.

She stopped in her brainstorm and took a look around her tidy kitchen with its new electric Frigidaire and Glenwood Ourway gas stove with its extra oven for baking bread. What an accomplishment for an Irish girl who had come to America with only the clothes on her back and a baby in her belly. It really was a shame that John Dodd couldn't have lived to see what Kitty had done for their family or that Mariah couldn't be around to enjoy these hard-earned rewards. Why, who better, then, to bring along on the company vacation than fellow Irishmen Peggy and Pickles McNichols?!

"Aw, now, Kitty," Peggy began, "me and the mister would love to join you and yours in Acey. But Maggie is about to give me another grandchild. Well, the doctor's saying there might be triplets in there. I promised I wouldn't turn into an apple and roll away from the Orange."

Kitty understood. She didn't know if she'd ever have other grandchildren, so she cherished the time she spent with Doris, enjoying the fine young lady she was turning into. Finding her a suitable husband was a concern, to be sure, but not just yet.

Still, Kitty was feeling expansive about an Atlantic City sojourn and believed the Dodds and Ryans should include some of their steadfast friends as part of their traveling entourage. Since John and Mary Monteverdi had been part of the family's adventures since before the days of *poitin* and Acme Chemical, perhaps they would like to take a long over-due vacation down the shore and check out the preparations for the island resort's 75th anniversary.

Sure enough, the Monteverdis were thrilled at Kitty's invitation to spend a week away.

"We just won a tidy sum in the Irish sweepstakes," Mary confided to Kitty. "I told John we should splurge. It's found money! This will be a lot of fun, all of us together. We'll talk to our son, Skip, and ask him to mind the store while we're gone. We might not get down there until Tuesday night. Will that be alright?"

"Oh, yes," Kitty replied. "We'll make sure you have a room next to ours."

When everyone had returned home, over supper Kitty laid out her proposal.

"We have two weeks to make reservations, arrange for time off for Doris from Drake Academy, check with Bobby Browne about that week's product run, let that nice young Dick Codey know the car won't be available…"

"Nobody better die while we're gone," Pete broke in.

"And," Kitty resumed, looking directly at her sons, "make sure nothing happens to your blind pig while we're away. We're not coming home to wind up in the pokey."

Better card players would not have been found that night than around the Dodds' table. But even as Frank and Pete solemnly nodded their heads, Frank's mind was racing ahead with a plan to surprise his mother and the rest of the family ~ if it worked. As soon as the table was cleared, he told Kitty he had to go see a man about a horse, and left the kitchen.

Once outside on Liberty Street, Frank walked up the hill to Danny Paris's house, and knocked on the door.

"Why Frankie, what a surprise," said Millie. "What brings you out this time of night?"

"Business, Millie, always business. Your husband around?"

"Of course he is. If I didn't know better, I'd say he was preparing the next batch of labels for Acme Chemical. Is that what you wanted to talk to him about?" she asked, leading Frank through the house, into the kitchen, and to a door that led to the cellar.

"Danny? Frank's here to see you. He's got his usual unusual request," she called down the stairwell, laughing.

It was nearly an all-day excursion that Monday, May 13th, to drive the Packard LeBaron down the coast road to Atlantic City. Doris caught a glimpse of the ocean once on the viaduct over the Raritan River. But it was a long stretch of macadam on Route 9 before the elevation dropped to sea level and the highway brought them over the Great Egg Harbor River Bridge. Doris looked east and saw where the river merged into the Great Bay. At the horizon line there was more blue water shimmering in the late afternoon sunlight.

"Smell the salt air, Doris?" Jim asked his daughter. "It's even better salt air than in Manasquan."

"Why is that?"

"There's more of it!"

An advanced phone call to his old Coast Guard buddy, Jimmy Sykes, had given Jim Ryan a heads up on the who's who expected in Atlantic City for that week. One of the men from the world of betting whom Jim most admired and wished he could meet was Moe Annenberg, publisher of the *Daily Racing Form*. Annenberg, it turned out, was traveling with Al Capone to attend a special conference in South Jersey. Jim said nothing to his wife nor brothers-in-law about his hunch. But were he to bet on their so-called business trip, he'd lay even money that Kitty chose the dates based on a hope and a prayer of meeting her hero. Jim was going to see what he could do to make both their wishes come true.

While no one phoned in a tip to the upper management at the Marlborough Blenheim Hotel, the experienced executives knew May 13 would be a day like no other. First there were the black limousines that Stu Wiser, general manager, noticed coming over the causeway on his drive to work. Then it was a fleet of limos – same ones? – that a hotel bellhop noticed making its way south, away from The Breakers, the resort's upper-crust hotel. Added to that, the hop witnessed Nucky Johnson, the city's power broker, bellowing in the middle of the avenue at a man a foot shorter than him with a scar slashed across his face. The man roared back his own brand of epithet-filled insults. Finally, Nucky shoved him back into his chauffer-driven car, and the line of limos continued to drive south on Pacific. Johnson was entertaining a rougher than usual crowd, the hop thought. He told Stu that most likely they wound up registered at one of the hotels around the Ritz-Carlton where Nucky had a residential suite.

But the real evidence that May 13 would be a day for the history books at the Marlborough Blenheim was the stack of telegrams and letters from captains of industry, foreign heads of state, and American politicians that sat in a staggering pile on Stu's desk. They were all addressed to a guest due to arrive that afternoon, in a party of six, with two more scheduled to arrive on Tuesday. Stu called in his second in command, Virginia McDowell, the leggy director of promotion and advertising the staff had nicknamed "Scissors".

"Gin, who are these people?" Stu asked. "Better yet, how does the staff address her?"

Stu passed across his desk a telegram from King Albert of Belgium written out to Princess Catherine. Next were two heavy-weight watermarked corporate envelopes, one from Detroit, the other from West Orange. Both were addressed to Madame Chairwoman Catherine K. Dodd of the Acme Chemical Corporation, Ltd.

In Gin's direction Stu next pushed a telegram from the Lord Mayor of Cork, Ireland, directed to Lady Kitty Dodd, followed by a cable from King George V for Dame Dodd, Order of the British Empire. The two last envelopes were addressed to the Honorable Catherine Dodd, Esq. One came from the office of New Jersey Governor Morgan F. Larson, the other from the White House, with President Herbert Hoover's stamped signature on the return line.

"Mrs. Dodd?" Gin suggested hopefully. "Do you want me to phone Dan Hennigan over at *The Press?* Or do you want to keep this on the Q.T.?"

Gin's approach to hotel publicity was unrivaled in Atlantic City. She especially enjoyed designing promotions around guests who wanted the public to know they were in residence at the Marlborough Blenheim. Gin had easily persuaded western movie star Tom Mix to pose with five children on a mounted horse on the beach in front of the hotel. Mix agreed to dress in his full cowboy regalia, with two six-shooters at his side (emptied of bullets, of course), and a lasso twirling overhead. That's where Gin wrote the words: "Teaching them the ropes." At the bottom of the ad she added the tag line: "You never know who you will ride with at the Marlborough Blenheim."

In a memorable magazine ad campaign, Gin arranged a photo shoot with Lassie and Rin Tin Tin, laying poolside with sunglasses, a comely waitress serving them umbrella drinks. The bubble above Rin Tin Tin carried the words: "They really know how to treat a movie star here at the Marlborough Blenheim." For Lassie Gin wrote: "Other places treat you like a dog." At the bottom of the page the copy read: "Your pet doesn't have to be famous to get first class treatment at the Marlborough Blenheim."

Just then the phone on Stu's desk rang.

"Yes? They are? We'll be right out." Turning to Gin Stu advised, "Call her Mrs. Dodd."

It felt good to get out of the LeBaron and stretch her legs. But for the life of her, Kitty couldn't understand the amount of solicitous attention the bellhops, the doormen, the concierge, the director of advertising and publicity, and the general manager, plus all the clerks behind the registration desk, were lavishing on her; the rest of her family, not quite as much. Is this how hotels operated in Atlantic City? Is this how the other half lived?

"Mrs. Dodd," Gin said. "It would be my extreme pleasure to show you, and your family, up to your suite."

"Suite?" Kitty shook her head. "My son-in-law reserved four rooms."

"Oh, Mrs. Dodd," Stu jumped in. "A woman of your standing in the international community deserves a suite; especially someone who does business with Thomas Edison, the man whose re-enforced concrete built The Blenheim. Because you are a friend of Mr. Edison's, we've arranged to put your party in the Wizard's Roost there. Really, Mrs. Dodd, it is our honor to have you be our guest this week. Gin?"

Stu motioned for Gin to escort the Dodd and Ryan entourage up the elevator to the six-sided suite just under the dome of the Blenheim's central tower. Each bedroom had views and French doors that opened to connecting balconies overlooking all of Absecon Island and the slate and turreted rooftops that gave the Queen of Resorts its famous skyline. Silver satin duvets were laid over the king-size beds. Unlike the single bath on Liberty Street the entire family had to share, each bedroom had an accompanying bathroom with fresh and salt water faucets and pink-and-black tiled showers separate from huge porcelain soaking tubs.

"Pinch me," Lil whispered to her husband.

The black-and-silver living room, anchored by a sinuous sofa and a small baby grand piano, had its own view and balcony overlooking the ocean. The dining room, with a view over the inlet, was outfitted with an ebony-lacquered table. An overflowing vase of deep rose cymbidium orchids and white roses commanded its center. In the fully equipped kitchen, an enormous welcome basket of fruit, Swiss chocolate, water crackers, canned sardines and *pâté de foie gras* sat squarely on the countertop.

Kitty was speechless.

"We've arranged for the Blenheim's executive chef, Frank D'Alonzo, to prepare a six-course French dinner here for you tonight," Gin said.

Kitty thought she was about to faint. Right then, the suite's doorbell sounded. Kitty gave a start. As she started to recognize the tune, "When Irish Eyes Are Smiling," Kitty began to relax a little. A smile appeared on her lips. As the melody played on, she broke into a soft chuckle. Then a laugh burbled up from somewhere deep inside of her until it burst from her throat. Her laughter swept her entire family up in its lilting sound. Everyone joined in to sing the chorus.

Satisfied, Gin opened the door.

"Jimmy!" Jim Ryan called out, and made his way over to the entry.

"Jim!"

The two men clapped each other on the back, and Jim turned to introduce his long-time friend, and a fellow bootlegger, to his extended family. Gin closed the door behind her and made her way downstairs to the kitchen to let Frank D'Alonzo know his special dinner guests were in residence.

Back in the suite's living room, Jimmy was explaining, "...that's right, there's a big gangster convention going on in town. They got thrown out of the WASP-only Breakers soon as the desk staff got a look at their mugs."

"Damnbrits!" Kitty, Frank, Pete, and Lil swore in unison.

Kitty then cleared her throat. Inquisitively she raised her eyebrows and slightly tilted her head to one side.

"So, there's a good chance we might run into one or two of them?"

Jimmy smiled.

"I've made reservations at the Silver Slipper Supper Club. You and Jim are my guests for dinner there tomorrow night. Food's pretty good. And, they put on quite a floor show. Maybe we'll spot someone you know," he added with a grin.

Between the long drive, Chef Frank's *bonne bouffe,* the salt air that found its way through the French windows left open during the night, everyone in the Wizard's Roost slept soundly into Tuesday morning. Frank was the first to get up, and within ten minutes of putting in a call to the front desk, the morning chef was up from the kitchen to prepare breakfast.

"Well, now, this won't do," Kitty protested. "We can go down and eat in the hotel restaurant with everyone else. Imagine all those guests who will go hungry without someone in the kitchen to make them rashers and bangers."

"Let's enjoy this for just a little longer," Frank pleaded. Changing the subject, he added, "After breakfast, we're going out to stroll the boards. Are you going to come with us?"

Kitty shook her head. An idea had occurred to her. The Boardwalk could wait. There was something else she wanted to do.

The late morning, then, found Frank, Pete, Lil, Jim, and Doris out on the vast wooden sidewalk, peering over the railing to watch sculptor Lorenzo Harris work his craft in the sand. A bucket for pitching coins was fitted into the scroll of an acanthus leaf that formed the grainy frame the black American artist had carved around his allegorical image of Bacchus, the god of wine. When Doris figured out what she was looking at, she clapped her hands in recognition of a greater realization: everything in Atlantic City was *in plain sight!* Nothing had to be hidden.

After tossing a couple of quarters into Harris's pail, the family walked over to the famous Steel Pier where among all the marquees for General Motors and bandleader John Philip Sousa, they noticed a young man walking with a sandwich board. The pier's famous diving horse, Red Lips, was going to jump at 11:30. Jim paid for admission to the pier, and the family made its way to the end of the long wharf, passing other amusements they might want to check out later, and found seats in the front row for the show.

Sitting last, on the end, Pete spotted the horse and rider first as they made their way towards the ramp. A soft ocean breeze picked up the ends of the rider's cinnamon brown curls and swirled them gently around her face. She shook her head to clear her vision, and Pete saw a pair of beautiful hazel eyes. The rider wore a blue wool one-piece bathing suit with a wide white belt cinched at her narrow waist. Slender legs gently gripped the spotted quarter horse she rode bareback. Firm hands held the reins. Up they went to the top of the platform. Pete and the rest of his family craned their necks to watch. A canned drum roll emitted from loud speakers set up behind them. Suddenly, without any announcement, the horse stepped over the edge of the platform, hurtling the female rider with him down forty feet into the salt water pool below. A collective gasp rose up from the crowd. The moment the splash was heard, a thunderous applause rose up to greet the horse and rider as they emerged from the water.

Pete was smitten. He leaned over to his brother. "I've got to meet that filly."

He hung around, waiting until Sonora Webster finished signing autographs. When the last photo op was over, Pete approached the rider and horse, and stuck out his beefy hand.

"Hi. I'm Pete Dodd," he said. "I think you're the bravest woman I've ever laid eyes on."

Sonora blushed, and offered her hand in return, shaking his with a firm grip.

"I used to be a boxer." Pete's words spilled out in a rush. "I own a bar now with my brother, Frank, up in north Jersey. We're down here for the week. Could I take you dancing tonight?"

Sonora's pretty face turned a becoming shade of pink. A soft Georgia drawl emerged from her bow-shaped lips.

"That's very sweet. I don't get much of a chance to go dancing, working all the time that I do," she said. "But I think it's only fair I tell you that you've got competition."

Pete hadn't thought of that.

"I could knock him out in three rounds, or less," he stoutly said. "Could you think it over? My offer to go dancing, that is. I heard at the front desk that there's dancing all night tonight on the Million Dollar Pier."

"And what front desk would that be?" she teased.

"We're stayin' at the Blenheim. In the Wizard's Roost. You know, it's named for Tom Edison."

Sonora Webster looked with new-found interest at Pete Dodd.

"I could meet you at the Million Dollar Pier tonight," she said. "Around eight? I'd love to go dancing."

Pete vigorously nodded his head.

"I have to go dry off now and prepare for the next dive," Sonora said, again extending her right hand.

Amazed at his good fortune, Pete clenched it a mite too tightly and Sonora winced. Immediately he loosened his grip. Then recalling the scene in front of Laird's distillery when his mother hired Bobby Browne, Pete brought Sonora's hand to his lips and kissed it.

"At eight."

Pete turned and walked with equal parts speed and determination, looking for his brother Frank. He found him, with the rest of the family, gathered in front of a miniature boxing ring under a hand-painted sign that said "Alley Cats". Everyone was laughing at two tabbies with tiny boxing gloves snugged on their front paws, taking swipes at each other.

"Frank, Frank," Pete tapped his brother's forearm with the backs of his fingers. "She said yes. Tonight at eight. We're cuttin' the rug!"

Pete's fair complexion was turning red in his excitement.

"Now all we have to do is find you a girl, and we can make this a foursome. Com' on."

Frank turned away from the cat fight just as the match was called. "I don't know, Pete. I'm kind of stuck on that Miss Reich from the Drake Academy."

"Aw com'on, Frankie. We're here for a week of fun in the sun where nobody knows us. Look at me, I just got a date with the star attraction of Atlantic City!"

Frank chuckled.

"Well, seeing as you booked the star, then who's left for me?"

From the Steel Pier the family ambled over to check out F.W.

Woolworth's famous lunch counter, and there the brothers made a new friend. Getting the last seat before the counter elbowed around, Frank struck up a conversation with the diner seated on the corner.

"What looks good today?" Frank asked, thinking the man's build made him look like a welter-weight fighter. The fellow had square shoulders, reddish brown hair, and steel-blue eyes.

"I hear the fried clams are pretty good," he answered, shaking his head, "but my budget is more in line with a grilled cheese and a root beer."

"Well," Frank said, holding out his hand "let me treat you. I'm here on a convention. Name's Frank Dodd."

"Name's Spencer Tracy. I'm here rehearsing."

"Rehearsing what, boxing?" Frank asked hopefully.

"Naw," Spencer said, "I'm in a show called 'Salt Water' at the Keith Theatre on Garden Pier. As soon as 'George White's Scandals' is done with its run, we move in."

"Oh, you're one of them actors," Frank said, warming to the subject of popular entertainment.

"Yup. I joined the Navy during the war, but never left the Norfolk Yards in Virginia," Spencer said. "I'm seeing the country from the footlights. Hell, maybe some day I'll see the world."

As Frank and Spencer started comparing notes between their Navy experiences, they discovered they also discovered their Irish backgrounds. Before too long, Pete joined in the conversation. By the time lunch was over, Doris's uncles saw to it that she had a souvenir picture taken with Spencer in the Woolworth photo booth to add to her scrap book.

Once back out on the Boardwalk, Pete, Frank, Jim, Lil, and Doris found themselves feeling a little drowsy and decided to go back to the Blenheim for an afternoon nap. The three men walked ahead, discussing where they might go to take in a little gambling action later than night. Lil and Doris walked at a slightly slower pace, absorbing as much of the thrilling Boardwalk atmosphere as they could when Doris spied the man who, in her words to her grandmother, "eats babies." She grabbed her mother's arm.

"Look, isn't that....," she asked, pointing across the boards.

Lil looked over and saw three men in suits approaching in their direction. One sported a red carnation in his lapel and a pair of owlish glasses on his nose. Next to him walked a slightly shorter man in a fedora, a scar clearly seen across his left check despite the attempt of an upturned coat collar to hide it. The third man hung back a little, surveying the crowd as they walked by.

Lil immediately grabbed Doris's wrist and pushed it down. "Yes, honey" and hurried her daughter up the boards to catch up with the men who had paused to light cigarettes by the Boardwalk rail.

"Al..." Lil hissed. "Al Capone. He's here. Are we going to tell Ma?"

Jim whirled around with a pleased look on his face that quickly disappeared when he caught his daughter's disapproving glance. Regaining his composure, he said, "Why don't we see what Jimmy Sykes can do tonight."

Kitty's absence on their Boardwalk adventures now was keenly felt. Her family began wondering what she had been up to while they were taking in some of the sights. This trip was her idea, after all. They hastened their walk back to the Blenheim. But once in the Wizard's Roost, they saw Kitty was not there. Frank picked up the suite's telephone and asked the switchboard to put him through to Virginia McDowell.

"Hiya, Gin, this is Frank Dodd. Yes, yes, we're having a grand time. We're back in the suite, but we don't see our mother here. There's no note. Would you happen to know where she might be?...

Yes. Yes…Okay, we'll be here. We're pretty bushed, and want to catch twenty winks. Okay. Thank you. Thanks."

In all her years in hospitality, "Scissors" McDowell never lost an important guest. Or even a minor one, for that matter. Until now. She picked up her telephone and dialed the front desk. Her brow furrowed. She called the concierge, Rick Ross. Her lips pursed. She pushed back from her desk and got up.

"She can't be…" Gin muttered, shaking her ash blond hair with its new peek-a-boo bangs and walked out of her office, turning away from the hotel lobby to go down a service corridor. At a pair of swinging doors marked "Staff Only" she pushed her way into the hotel pantry and continued walking until she found herself in the hotel kitchen.

What she saw brought her to a full stop. There, at the prep table, stood Kitty Dodd, in a hotel apron already embroidered with her name, kneading bread dough. A gallon of buttermilk stood to one side, along with a bowl of measured sugar. Across the counter stood the pastry staff, following Kitty's lead, each kneading dough. Utterly captivated by her lyrical brogue, everyone listened with rapt attention as Kitty spooled out the story about hijacking the British supply wagons in Ireland. Noticing Gin McDowell seemingly rooted in place, Kitty called over to her.

"There, now, Miss McDowell, you're just in time for tea. We're about to put our loaves to bake in the ovens. You'll have them fresh to serve at dinner."

Gin sputtered. "Mrs. Dodd…Mrs. Dodd…what a…ah… surprise to find you in our kitchen. I hope this doesn't mean you don't like our food."

"Oh, quite the contrary. I came down with the breakfast chef after finding out no one knew how to make soda bread," Kitty said, smiling. "I offered to show everyone how easy it is."

Gin slowly nodded with the dawning realization that for all the acclaim Mrs. Dodd received in those welcoming letters and telegrams, and the luxury she encountered in the Wizard's Roost, Kitty Dodd missed the comforting routine of what was familiar to her.

"Mrs. Dodd, I have an idea," she said, walking over to put her arm around her guest's shoulders. "The Monteverdis, your other guests, will be arriving shortly. How about I schedule you, your daughter, granddaughter, and Mrs. Monteverdi for a "Day of Beauty" at our new Helena Rubenstein spa. On us. It will be our thanks for the cooking lesson. Let us help ease you into the Atlantic City lifestyle…."

Now it was Kitty's turn to be surprised.

"Why, that's very generous of you," she started, but was stopped by the applause that broke out from the kitchen staff. "Well, alright. I think so. Yes. I would like to try that."

"Let me have your apron," Gin said. "We'll get it cleaned and pressed so you can take it home at the end of your week here."

Kitty obliging took the apron from around her neck and handed it over. Gin offered Kitty her arm and began to walk her out of the kitchen. Just as they got to the pantry, Kitty turned around and called out to the staff, "Don't leave the bread in too long. Every oven is different. If the bread bakes too fast, the outside will be crusty, but the inside will be too doughy." With a final wave of her hand, Kitty fell into step with the long legs of Scissors McDowell, and tried to keep up.

By the time the Blenheim's special guests had finished their day of beauty, quite a transformation had taken place, especially with Kitty. Gone was her snow white hair. Convinced by Doris to get a color rinse and a modern cut, Kitty's locks had the redwood color of her youth and a shape that, with a little pomade, swept the thick waves away from her face to bring out the bright blue of her eyes that time had not dimmed. Her nails were manicured in a blush pink, her skin massaged and powdered, and a faint scent of lavender gently emanated from her as she walked.

"Oh, Grandma!" Doris exclaimed, thrilled over Kitty's new appearance. "Now we have to get you some new clothes!"

Once again Kitty started to protest, but Lil and Mary Monteverdi intervened.

"It's time," Lil said. "No more widow's weeds for you."

"I noticed a sign for Maîson Fernande as I came to join you at the spa," Mary added. "Why don't we go see what she has?"

The four women made their way through the lobby until they found themselves in front of two separate plate glass display windows, divided by a center door. In the left window, between the two mannequins dressed in short hemlines and boa feathers, hung a discrete sign:

"Glamour is what makes a man ask for your telephone number."

In the right window, between a mannequin outfitted in a trouser dress and another in a brightly beaded frock, another sign read:

"Glamour is what makes a woman ask for the name of your dressmaker."

Inside, clothing filled the racks like a well-stocked designer showroom ready for the catwalk in Paris or Milan. From simple day clothes in jersey knits and leather to evening dresses in lamé, metallic lace, and rhinestone-embroidered chiffon, Kitty was overwhelmed by the dazzling array of choices. She didn't have the first idea of how to go about making a selection.

Just then Fernande Chapon materialized from the dressing rooms to survey her clients.

"*Oui, Mesdames*," she said. "How may I be of assistance?"

Gratefully, the women yielded to Fernande's expert eye and after a couple of hours they emerged carrying small shopping bags of jewelry accessories. They agreed with Fernande's suggestion that a bellhop deliver their boxes and clothing bags of newly purchased dresses in a luggage caddy to their suite. Kitty consented to several tailored suits from famed Parisian designer Coco Chanel. Lil selected a number of light, floral dresses from Jeanne Lanvin. Mary chose the new prêt a porté couture from the House of Worth. And all the women decided to buy a couple of extra pieces for Doris, especially after she swooned at the exotic outfits from Erté.

"You get tickets from *Mademoiselle Virginie*," Fernande said, "and see the costumes *R.T.* designed for 'George White's Scandals' at the Keith. *Trés chic*."

With a royal navy blue dress made of buttery jersey that flattered her figure and a triple-strand of cream-colored Chanel pearls, the crystal-encrusted Art Deco clasp fashionably showing at the side of her throat, Kitty placed herself between Jim Ryan and Jimmy Sykes and walked out of the Blenheim. The cab ride from Ohio to Kentucky Avenue didn't take long. In front of the Silver Slipper, the trio again linked arms and walked into the supper club. It took but a moment for Kitty's eyes to adjust to the intimately lit interior, where wisps of cigarette smoke mingled with the tiny light beams that shown down from the ceiling. Immediately recognizing Jimmy Sykes, one of club's frequent patrons, the maître d' led them to a large round table near the stage that was just ordering a round of drinks. Kitty noted three empty chairs. They were not together.

One was beside a thin man in pinstripes wearing glasses that Kitty thought made him look like an accountant. Jimmy introduced him as the publisher of the *Daily Racing Forum*, and Jim Ryan immediately stuck out his hand in greeting, and then sat down beside Moe Annenberg.

Kitty next noticed the table's only woman, a brassy blond with a fawn-colored mink cape draped over one shoulder who reclined in the arm of a freshly shaven man who wore his hair slicked back. Next to them sat a man with thick black wavy hair parted on his left side; a friendly smile slowly spread across his face as he sized up Kitty. Also at the table were the two businessmen Kitty had met in Newark four weeks ago, Longie Zwillman and Dutch Schultz. She held their gaze. Longie, the only one outfitted in a white dinner jacket, elbowed Dutch, acknowledging the pecking order at this table.

Dutch stood up. "How nice of you to join us," he said.

He turned to acknowledge the cherubic-faced man to his left who was taking a cigar out of his mouth with his left hand.

"Mrs. Dodd, I presume," Al Capone said, rising from his chair. "Won't you join us and bring some class to this table of clowns."

Male laughter rippled around the table.

"And, perhaps a little marital advice to the newlyweds, Anna and Meyer Lansky."

More laughter followed as Al pulled out the chair next to him and indicated it was for Kitty.

What a well-mannered young man, Kitty said to herself. I knew his mother brought him up right. The newspapers had it all wrong about him.

"I understand we're both in the delivery business," he said after Kitty put her napkin in her lap.

"Yes, Mr. Capone. That's true. You and I supply the public with a product they demand."

"Please call me Al, Mrs. Dodd," he responded.

"Please, Al, call me Kitty," she replied.

Chuckles from Kitty's new friends helped further to break the ice. As the evening got underway, Kitty found herself relaxing in the company of her peers – immigrant working people who had achieved the American Dream. She was seated at a table that not only included her hero, Al Capone, but also Lucky Luciano, the conference's chairman of the board, equally at home with a copy of Standard & Poor's as with a Smith & Wesson. Oh, and those two beer bootleggers she met in the back room of the Palace Chop House in Newark, Longie and Dutch; they weren't so fierce-looking in the casual, resort atmosphere that was Atlantic City. In fact, they were down right friendly, Kitty decided.

As Jimmy had promised, the food was good: Delmonico steaks, baby peas, puréed potatoes; plenty of beer and wine to slake every thrist. The floor show featured the newest singing and dancing sensation, Ruth Andrae and her S.S. Vogues. It was a heady evening, filled with bonhomie. *So this is how the high rollers live, Kitty thought.*

As the hour approached midnight, Al offered to see her back to the Blenheim. Kitty looked across the table to the two men who had made this evening possible. Jim and Jimmy nodded their heads.

Once inside his limo, Al told his driver to take them all the way to the Boardwalk and, once there, to hail them a rolling chair.

"Ever been in one of these, Kitty?" he asked.

"No. As a matter of fact, tonight is the first time I've left the hotel since we arrived."

"No fooling?" he asked, offering Kitty his arm so she could climb into the double-wide wicker chair. "My wife would have been out first day here with our son, making sure he got some fresh air."

The big man paused and then spoke so low Kitty had to lean

in to hear him above the rhythmic clicking of the chair's wheels as they rolled across the boards.

"I miss them," he said. "Sonny especially. He's eleven. If I have to do time to make peace with the conference, it's going to be hard....It would have been easier if we had had a girl...but then I wouldn't have married Mae. She did give me a son, though, and that's what I wanted, so I married her. Can you blame me?"

Kitty gently patted his arm.

"Girls can give you their own brand of heartache, Al," she said. "Boys can, too. I know. I've raised two of them."

"So you know how hard it can be," he said. "Sometimes you can get much farther with a kind word and a gun than you can with a kind word alone."

"Other times," Kitty chuckled softly, "you have to give them territories so they can find their own way in their own time."

Al smiled in the moonlight.

"Speaking of fresh air, you ought to ask that Jimmy Sykes to take you out on an ocean boat ride. We went to a rum party the other night on the *Well Deserved.* In another couple of nights, the floating party is going to be aboard *That's My Hon.*"

Just then the chair pulled up to the Blenheim's Boardwalk entrance.

"Pretty nice digs you put up in, Kitty," he said. "The business must be good to you. Maybe I'll stop in for a cup of tea before I go."

"Sure, Al. If there's anything you want to talk over, I'm here all week."

Al climbed out of the chair and turned to help Kitty alight on the boards. He handed the chair's pusher a hundred-dollar bill. With a tilt of his head, Capone indicated to the young man to scram. Abruptly, he turned his chair around and pushed it in the direction of the Traymore Hotel.

"Good night, Mrs. Dodd," Al said, taking her right hand in his, and gently closing his left over it.

"Good night, Mr. Capone. It was a pleasure to meet you."

Jock Sanders stood in the deep shadows of the arches that fronted the massive Moorish-styled building that was the Traymore, impatiently waiting for the now empty rolling chair to return with the information he paid for. No more than twenty years old, the sinewy driver pulled abreast of Jock and stopped, pretending to check the chair's wheels.

"Well?" Jock hoarsely whispered.

The young man held out his hand.

"I already paid you."

"You didn't pay me to drop a dime. Only to pick them up. You wanna know where she's going Saturday night, you gotta pay up."

Fuming, Jock rooted around in his pockets until he found a money clip. Extracting a fifty dollar bill, he handed it over.

"This is going to cost you double on account you'll be in clover when you drop the net."

Exasperated, Jock unfolded another Ulysses Grant.

"They're going out to Rum Row. *That's My Hon*, that's a boat. Pleasure doing bidness." With that, the young man turned away and started whistling a tune to attract new rolling chair customers who wanted to be pushed along in the romantic moonlight. Had Jock known the words, perhaps he would have joined in:

How dry I am, how dry I am
It's plain to see just why I am
No alcohol in my highball
And that is why so dry I am.

Another heaven-sent morning rose up over the Atlantic to greet the Dodds and the Ryans. The spring air was warming up, an indicator that summer was coming. The women decided to let the men sleep off their evening of dancing, drinking, and making business deals, and on their own explore the length of the Boardwalk. Added Lil, "They're probably going to want to try a little more gambling today anyway."

"Let's take a jitney," Doris suggested.

Kitty looked in mock shock at her granddaughter's easy willingness to spend money.

"Let's take the trolley so we can sightsee along the way," Kitty countered.

The women decided to go all the way up to Massachusetts Avenue and start their morning by touring the Heinz Pier. Promoted by the late H.J. as his Crystal Palace by the Sea, the wharf featured the Pittsburgh company's 57 varieties of canned and bottled foods from horseradish and ketchup to pickles and steak sauce. Especially, the pickles. Once at the pier, Kitty decided she would get a pickle pin to bring home to Peggy McNichols. Touring the exhibit, the women oohh-ed and aahh-ed over the rustic French demonstration kitchen and its samples, skipped the English country hearth exhibit entirely, and noted some ideas for future home renovations from the modern kitchen display. With Mary Monteverdi in the lead, they examined the art and decorative objects that filled the solarium before Doris announced she was hungry.

"The salt air must be doing you some good," Lil commented. Indeed, the healthy air was a boon to all the women. By not staying in the sun too long their cheeks glowed from the sunshine and they could feel themselves invigorated by their tour of the Boardwalk. It was a welcomed break from their routine in the Oranges.

"How would you all like to eat a lobster?" asked Mary, remaining true to her role as the wife of a food importer. "Let's walk up to the channel. My husband told me we should have the Hackney half-lobster experience. Half if you only half like it."

Emboldened by their collective experiences in sampling the high life in Atlantic City, the women were all in agreement to try seafood and pretty soon they found themselves walking past an enormous fish tank filled with warring black-shelled crustaceans, their antennae waving wildly in the water as they used their claws to snap at each other and anyone who came near the glass. Doris couldn't keep her eyes off the beasts. Neither could Kitty.

"We're going to eat those?" she asked incredulously.

Mary laughed and led them into the vast restaurant where they were seated at a table overlooking the water. Before long they found themselves dressed in bibs, nut crackers in one hand and delicate pick forks for extracting the white meat from the cooked orange-red shells in the other hand.

"Oh, this is goooood," Doris said enthusiastically, dipping a piece of lobster meat into a ramie cup of clarified butter. "Daddy should come here and try this."

Kitty and other the women nodded in agreement. This was a restaurant experience worth sharing with the men. To walk off their lunch, the women returned to the Boardwalk and made their way down to Garden Pier.

"Isn't that the show Madame Fernande told us to get tickets for?" Lil asked, reading the B.F. Keith Theatre marquee for "George White's Scandals".

The women read the fine print. Sure enough, the type read: costumes by Erté.

"I wonder who these men are?" mused Kitty, pointing to the names of Irving Caesar, George White, and Cliff Friend.

"We'll ask when we get back to the hotel," Lil said.

"Here's Spencer Tracy." Doris pointed to the marquee window where the banner headline read: "Coming Attractions."

"Wasn't he just dreamy?"

"OK," said Lil, "we're not staying in Atlantic City long enough for you to take up with an actor!"

"My heavens," Kitty exclaimed. "Look over there."

Through an open doorway, the women saw what looked like an enormous typewriter key. As they moved closer to the exhibition room they noticed more keys. Doris began reading out loud from a sign:

"This Underwood typewriter is the largest in the world! It weighs 14 tons. It stands 18 feet high."

The No. 5 model was massive.

"Oh, take a picture of me with it so I can show Miss Reich," Doris asked, handing her Kodak Brownie to her mother that she remembered to take with her from the Wizard's Roost that morning. "Come on, Grandma, you get in, too."

Kitty marveled at the promotional display, silently absorbing all that was happening to her. Between meeting Al Capone, seeing Doris's look of delight at eating a lobster, watching her daughter relax, and enjoying Mary's company, this corporate retreat was exceeding far beyond what Kitty could have imagined.

A little later, as the ladies made their way across the Blenheim's richly marbled lobby, the concierge, Rick Ross, called out to them, rising up from his desk.

"Miss McDowell was called away. She asked that I take of you and left me these envelopes to give out," he said. One had Lil and Jim's name on it. A second said Mary and John Monteverdi. The third had Kitty's name and was the thickest. As Kitty opened her envelope, Rick started to explain.

"Four years ago Irving Chase stayed with us here in the Blenheim and enjoyed our traditional English high tea service. He used our lobby piano to write the song 'Tea for Two'," Rick explained. "Gin heard the song was a favorite with Frank and Doris. She was able to get four tickets for the new show he wrote that's winding up its run at the Garden Pier."

"Frank will be pleased, I'm sure," Kitty said as Doris clapped her hands. A night out with her uncles was bound to produce some hijinx afterwards, and she was sure her grandmother, with her new look and adventurous attitude, would go along with anything her uncles proposed.

"Mrs. Monteverdi," Rick was saying, "you hold everyone's passes for tomorrow night's 'Hot Chocolate Revue' featuring New Orleans trumpeter Louis Armstrong at Nixon's Apollo Theatre."

Lil opened her envelope and saw four tickets.

"Your husband asked for those," Rick explained. "Mae West is at the Globe and he wanted to take you to see her in 'Diamond Lil'. Tonight is the only night we could get tickets. She's sold out. Mr. Ryan has invited the Monteverdis to join you."

Lil smiled, a rush of feeling coming over her as she recognized her husband's sentimental streak. For the second time since arriving in Atlantic City, Lil found herself saying, "Pinch me."

Chapter 7: The Pursuit of Happiness

Not one usually given to premonitions, Kitty took her morning cup of tea to the dining room's balcony and looked out over Atlantic City. At mid-morning, the resort teemed with activity. Kitty noted delivery trucks making their way to restaurants and hotels with Thursday deliveries. Down Pacific Avenue she saw tradesmen feverishly working to finish the new buildings scheduled to open for the resort's official 75th gala anniversary. Kitty realized a train must have pulled into the station as she saw the long line of taxi cabs quickly whisking away groups of men in bowler hats, leather sports jackets, and bright green ties. Looking west, Kitty's eyes finally spotted what she had been hoping not to see: a lone black limousine slowly heading across the causeway. Even before the doorbell to the Wizard's Roost rang, Kitty knew she'd never see Al Capone again. He had made a courageous decision, Kitty thought, and she sent up a silent prayer to keep the big man safe while he stayed in the big house.

Frank walked into the suite's dining room and Kitty turned away from the balcony to approach her son. Silently he handed over an envelope. Al's note inside was simple:

Current conditions won't last. Find new ways to expand your brand of better living. With admiration, Al

Kitty looked at her son, a gentle maternal smile emerging on her lips and at the corners of her eyes. Frank, Pete, Lil, and especially Doris, were her future. Could she find new opportunities in Atlantic City that would enable her to expand the Dodd's family business into legitimate brands when the time came?

Frank's voice broke into her thoughts.

"Gin McDowell left word she's got another tour lined up for us. That woman has been working overtime! Lil and the rest of the gang went out early for breakfast on the boards, but they're going to join us. Pete and I'll wait for you to get ready."

Kitty nodded. Here was an entire city bursting with all kinds of possibilities, where business didn't have to be hidden, where entertainment was top-of-line, and fascinating people from all walks of life were just waiting to be met. Surely in this intoxicating mix new connections could be made. While Kitty acknowledged she had promised her family, and also Gin McDowell and Mary Monteverdi, to relax and have fun, Al Capone was right: whenever the ineffective Prohibition Act was repealed, the family had to be ready to move in a new direction.

Kitty realized it was getting late in the morning. *Time's a-going by, she thought.* Within the hour Kitty was dressed and coiffed, choosing a beautiful powder blue suit with gold braid trim, custom-made by Madame Fernande. Mary had insisted Kitty treat herself to a light wool crepe ensemble that she could mix-and-match with other pieces in her newly expanding wardrobe. The suit came with a white bib collar blouse and a flattering hat in blue, gold, and white. It was an ideal outfit for making a good first impression.

When Kitty and her sons stepped off the Blenheim's elevator and into the lobby, they found themselves in the midst of an enormous crowd of men, sporting the same bright green neckties Kitty had observed coming out of the train station. The excitement level was high, particularly around a tight circle of older men. As Kitty and her sons slowly moved into the lobby, the black suits hovering in lines before the registration desk parted to let her pass at the same time that the knot of men loosened and fanned out around one individual in particular. Suddenly, Kitty found herself face to face with the smooth, grinning face of a man who looked like he had stepped out of a magazine advertisement for men's shaving cream, Barbasol. Frank and Pete sharply drew in their breaths. Here, right in front of them, was the legendary All-American football player and now celebrated coach of Notre Dame University; the man who invented the forward pass. The man's own blue eyes locked on Kitty's and he instinctively held out his right hand. Equally mesmerized by the friendly Norwegian face staring at her, Kitty stretched out her own hand to meet his.

"Knute Rockne, m'am," he said. "You must be a real Notre Dame fan. In that blue and gold you look like the new statue of the Madonna we just installed on the dome of our main building."

"Kitty Dodd," she responded, flattered and not a little self-conscious as she heard the noticeable drop in sound throughout the vast marble lobby as everyone strained to eavesdrop on their conversation.

Turning to the man standing next him, Knute said, "Barry, I think Kitty Dodd's presence is an omen. We should invite her to tomorrow night's dinner. With her there, the alumni chapter could raise a lot of money for new campus construction."

Barry O'Connor eagerly nodded in agreement; on his shoulders rested the challenge of besting other alumni chairmen around in the country in raising money for their alma mater. "On behalf of the Notre Dame Alumni Chapter of New York-New Jersey-and-Philadelphia, it would be an honor to have you join the Fighting Irish for dinner and entertainment in the Wedgewood Room."

"I'd be delighted," Kitty said, seizing on the opportunity to try her luck at networking with this crowd of university athletes-turned-businessmen. This kind of gamble was right up her alley. "But I don't go anywhere without my chaperones."

Kitty smiled sweetly, indicating Frank and Pete who stood on either side of her, their jaws slightly agape, amazed at what was happening in front of them. The brothers simultaneously proffered their right hands.

"Barry O'Connor," said the Notre Dame alumnus, shaking each hand, in turn. "I'm the chapter president. Welcome. Welcome. Welcome. I'll gladly set aside three tickets for the Dodd family for tomorrow night. We look forward to having you as our guests."

Invigorated by the possibilities of what Friday night might yield, Kitty led her sons on a brisk walk out of the hotel. It was Frank who had to direct them to the right when they exited the Blenheim. For the first time since she had arrived in Atlantic City, Kitty found herself taking in the sights that were south of their hotel: first there came the sprawling Hotel Dennis with its ornate French Empire roof, then followed the boxy brick-clad Shelburne Hotel. After that came a cathedral-like edifice whose exterior was lined in colorful terra cotta tiles and where a swarm of workmen were assembling what looked like a theater billboard. Next came a series of one and two-story buildings whose glass fronts promoted souvenirs from far away: Mr. Lim had knick knacks from the Orient; Madame Zelda learned the ancient art of fortune-telling in Transylvania; S.S. Adams brought you magic tricks from four continents.

Hovering just beyond this stretch of retail, Kitty saw what looked like an enormous building whose curved roof resembled a beer cask. Kitty had never seen anything this gigantic in her entire life. Why, it probably dwarfed the Cathedral of St. Mary and St. Anne back in her native Cork. Neither Lillian McNamara's account nor the *Newark News* photos had done justice to the $15 million jubilee hall whose design was a combination of Roman Revival and Art Deco stylings. Where workmen on scaffolds were chiseling the Atlantic City credo on the Indiana limestone façade, Kitty saw the rest of the family waiting. Jim Ryan and John Monteverdi were talking with a well-dressed man who radiated warmth and a kind of stage presence that Kitty couldn't quite identify. Was he an actor? Jim spoke first, making the introductions.

"This is Joe Amiel, radio host of 'Atlantic City After Hours' on WPG. He's going to be our tour guide!"

"What a pleasure to meet you," Joe said. "Your son-in-law has been filling me in on how this is your first visit to the Queen of Resorts. Welcome. Welcome. Welcome. I'm thrilled to take you around and show off our one-of-a-kind convention hall and the new studios of WPG."

Kitty followed Joe into the radio station's Spanish-styled reception room, complete with a tiled fountain and tapestries that hung on the walls. She paid close attention as he continued his patter.

"We've got the latest in radio technology, a generation ahead of what we have on the Steel Pier. The engineers say the broadcasts' overspill will reach people from Maine to Florida! We start airing

May 31, just a couple of weeks from now.

"With all the bookings the hall has for conventions and pageants and musical performances, I'll be interviewing every entertainer and captain of industry that comes through here. I'm hoping to get Thomas Edison when the National Electric Light Association officially opens the hall next month. But they say he's become a recluse. So we might get Henry Ford instead!" he added, breathlessly.

"Tell me, Joe, who pays for your broadcasts?" Kitty asked, motioning for Doris to come closer.

"Well, as you may know WPG stands for the 'World's Playground.' Our sponsors want to be a part of that tag line for Atlantic City. So, they are restaurants, hotels, theaters, and with the new hall, companies that will come here to present at industrial trade shows."

With Al's advice to look for future opportunities fresh in her mind, Kitty felt she was on to something.

"Could WPG have a radio show devoted to women's issues that..." she paused, "could be sponsored by the Drake Academy for Progressive Young Women?"

Joe nodded sagely.

"I don't see why not. Women listen to radio as much as men do. Probably even more," he added with a chuckle.

"That's good to know, don't you think so, Doris?"

Doris agreed, surprised at how quickly her grandmother seized up the potential in this growing medium of radio.

With Joe leading the way, the Dodds, Ryans and Monteverdis spent the next several hours in awe, meeting various crews which were hard at work to finish the ultra modern facility in time for its June ribbon-cutting ceremony.

"It's much grander than any of the armories we've been in,"

Pete observed.

"We've got features in this building no other city in the world has!" boasted Joe. "We're having a special organ built with more than 30,000 pipes. It will produce sound that will fill this entire room" he added, sweeping both his arms overhead in large circular arcs.

The special, innovative touches were mind-boggling. Kitty, Lil, Doris, and Mary marveled that compressed sugar cane was used for the 196,000-square-foot ceiling's acoustic tiles. Frank was impressed that the barrel ceiling was lined in painted aluminum to better reflect light. Pete and John walked around the perimeter of the concrete floor, discussing what kind of sports might be played simultaneously on its seven acres, and quickly decided that a combination of ice hockey and boxing could be just the ticket.

Overwhelmed and a little hungry from absorbing the dizzying array of information during their tour of Convention Hall, the families decided to go their separate ways to recuperate. They met up later at Nixon's Apollo Theatre to hear Louis Armstrong in the Broadway-bound "Hot Chocolate Revue." Afterwards, Jimmy Sykes joined them for dancing on the Millionaire Dollar Pier where Pete was over the moon to discover Sonora Webster there, who was hoping to see him again. The Monteverdis surprised everyone when they joined in the line dance for the latest interpretation of the Charleston. Not to be outdone, Jim and Lil stepped it up for the Lindy Hop.

Frank invited Doris to be his partner for the swing-out version of the Lindy. As uncle and niece moved around the dance floor, Frank decided to ask Doris how she would feel if he pursued the director of the Drake Academy.

"I'll run after her until she catches me."

Kitty's introduction to the new medium of radio and its possibilities for programming and sponsorships as a new way to make money whetted her appetite. On Friday morning, Gin arranged for special admission to a new theater about to open on the Boardwalk at Arkansas Avenue. What made this behind-the-scenes look extra special was that it included the sound check of a talking picture, Alfred Hitchcock's latest suspense film, "Blackmail."

" 'Broadway Melody' won the Oscar for best picture last night,' Gin explained to everyone. "We hope to get that here for the jubilee's summer crowds. But 'Blackmail' is Alfred's go at a talkie and I think you might enjoy being the first patrons to hear it."

Gin went on to tell everyone how theater impresario Stanley Warner had sunk $2.7 million into sculpting a Moorish-inspired showroom. Kitty and Doris were agog when they heard it sat 4,300, with a parterre and mezzanine level, just like in a theater where live performances took place. The floors were tiled terrazzo. Gilt-framed mirrors lined the lobby.

"So this is what the men were working yesterday when we walked by," Kitty noted.

Once inside, everyone was speechless. They settled into plush seats upholstered in patterned velvet and watched overhead as twinkling stars in the frescoed ceiling dimmed into twilight and then no light at all as the room plunged into darkness. The curtain went up, and Pathé newsreels flashed across the screen with subtitles, separated by frames that identified each news segement's sponsor.

Bell Laboratories invents the first color television: RCA Radio and Victor Records

W.A. Morrison introduces first quartz-crystal clocks for precise time-keeping: Atlantic City the World's Playground

Museum of Modern Arts Opens in New York City: Jack Dempsey's Steakhouse

Inauguration of 31st president Herbert Hoover: Canada Dry, Philadelphia's distributor of choice for 'the champagne of ginger ales'.

"Never forget we voted for Al Smith," Kitty whispered to Doris. "He could have been America's first Catholic president."

The screen went black and then from sound amplifiers in the four corners of the vast theater were heard the sounds of a wheel turning. Slowly, an image emerged on the screen and after a few moments it was clear that a tire was turning in a counter-clockwise motion. As the story unfolded, sounds of a piano playing, a bird chirping, and occasional bits of dialogue emanated from the strategically placed speakers. The effect haunted Kitty. Or, maybe it was the film's plot. Alice White was blackmailed for a murder she may, or may not, have committed. The accusation reminded Kitty of the British naval officers on Hawlbowline Island and their assumption that Mrs. O'Shea was at fault for ruining Irish efforts to get their independence.

Being in a business that is too connected to the dark side of authority isn't good for the long haul, Kitty mused. We need to find a way to convert Acme Chemical and The Place into legitimate enterprises.

Late that afternoon as her daughter and granddaughter helped her dress for the Notre Dame dinner, Kitty realized belatedly that she hadn't thought to ask for tickets for the Dodd women.

"Oh, don't worry about us, Ma," Lil said. "Atlantic City has plenty of ways to keep us entertained while you mix it up with the hoi polloi. Me and Jim are thinking about taking Doris over to Bader Field for a ride with that stunt pilot we've heard so much about, Gary Chrisman."

"Someday that university will take in women," Kitty continued with her train of thought. "Not in my lifetime. And not in time for

Doris. But eventually. You mark my words."

"What?! You becoming one of those women who can see into the future?" Lil teased her mother as she and Doris put the finishing touches on Kitty's outfit. From the Erté purchases at Maison Fernande, they had selected a paisley print in blue and seafoam green with tiny yellow accents that was done up as a flowing, floor-length wrap dress with a white corded sash. The shawl collar and wide cuffs were made from white satin. Around her neck Kitty put the Chanel necklace she had fallen in love with. With a little more persuasion, she agreed to wear the matching white satin turban that glittered with a crystal pendant at its center.

When Kitty, Frank, and Pete arrived in the lobby, their timing couldn't have been more perfect. Here was the Fralinger String Band, fronted by the blond-haired Jablonski twins from the Oranges. Frank and Pete were overjoyed to see their childhood chums!

"Come on! Come on!" the sisters cried. "We've choreographed a special Mummer's Strut in honor of the Fighting Irish. We're leading the band into the Wedgewood Room! We heard you're the guests of honor!"

As the tune "Oh dem golden slippers" began to play, Kitty, Frank, and Pete fell into formation right behind the accordion-wielding sisters, mimicking their every foot move and hand gesture as the merry parade made its way through the elevated walkway from the Blenheim into the Marlborough, and downstairs into the famous glass-domed circular banquet hall.

What a spread! Green and blue napkins alternated on the white linen tabletops. Porcelain plates and crystal goblets were rimmed in gold. The men, some who looked like fresh graduates who had just played football a year before, and older alums with distinguishing grey at their temples, were all handsomely attired and, Kitty noticed, radiated success. Frank and Pete fit right in with their newly purchased black dinner jackets and trousers with black satin stripes running down the outer seams. On advice from Gin McDowell, the pair had even made a special purchase of green silk neckties.

Sitting at the head table, Barry O'Connor was master of ceremonies. In his opening remarks he thanked Knute Rockne for flying in all the way from Indiana to attend this special dinner designed to raise funds so the university could continue to expand.

"As part of that tactical art of persuading you to part with your profits, Coach Rocke has brought some special friends with him," Barry added. "Coach, would you do the honors?"

Knute went to the microphone, thanked Bill for his hospitality, and proceeded to introduce New York City Mayor Jimmy Walker.

"Even though he's a Jesuit scholar, let's give him a rousing Order of the Holy Cross welcome."

Applause dutifully went up from the crowd.

"It's true, I'm a Jesuit," Walker said as he got to the microphone. "But the brothers at Xavier High School couldn't hold me back from singing in public and dancing on the stage."

Hoots erupted from around the Wedgewood Room.

The dapper mayor, with a three-point handkerchief in the breast pocket of his double-breasted suit, carried on for a while, promising to belt at least one number before the night was over – "Or, you can put a little extra money in a bowler hat so I won't sing!" - and then he introduced heavyweight champion and entrepreneur Jack Dempsey who had come down on the train with him.

"Thank you, Jimmy. It's always interesting to see what kind of get-up you're going to arrive in," Jack said. "I see you left the spats and top hat up at home. You must think you're on vacation in Atlantic City. You know Knute brought you here to work!"

Laughter erupted around the room in which there wasn't an empty seat to be had. Kitty was amazed at the gathering of well-connected Notre Dame alumni and just as impressed with the line-up on the dais that happened to include Gin McDowell and Joe Amiel.

"Now I want to introduce you to a man who's the youngest amongst us, Baby, ah Babe Ruth."

At 34 years old, the beefy Babe, of the well-chronicled endless appetites, was the youngest athlete at the head table. Jack was the old man at 46. But instead of taking on the boxing champ, Babe unleashed his coarse tongue on Notre Dame's beloved football coach, who at 41, was a trim, compact man who looked like he could still play end and throw a forward pass with ease.

"See these legs?" Ruth said, grabbing a hold of one of his meaty thighs clothed in a dark pinstripe serge. "I bet they can kick a pigskin farther than those twigs you stand on!"

Like a slingshot, a growling murmur made it way around the banquet hall.

Babe looked over at Knute. Knute raised his eyebrows into his high forehead and receding hairline.

"I'll bet a thousand dollars on it for your alumni fund!" For added emphasis, Ruth banged his hand on the banquet table and then abruptly sat down.

Immediately Gin McDowell jumped up and swiftly made her way over to the microphone. "The Marlborough Blenheim will donate a thousand dollars to the Notre Dame alumni fund to see this contest tomorrow at noontime on the front lawn of the hotel."

Another rumbled reaction rose up from the diners.

Swept up in the impromptu contest, Frank leapt from his seat beside Kitty to join Gin at the podium.

"Acme Chemical of the Oranges will put up another thousand!"

Kitty beamed from her seat. Her company was getting some favorable attention thanks to this unplanned opportunity.

Not wanting to be left out of the competition, Joe Amiel hastily made his way to the mic to join Gin and Frank.

"WPG Radio will add another thousand dollars and the right to interview the contestants when the match is over!"

At that, the room erupted in cheers and applause. Additional shout-outs with offers of more money to be added to the fund-raising pot resounded around the hall. With a big grin on his face, Barry O'Connor was clearly proud of his fellow alumni and the new friends Notre Dame made that night.

At 11:45 a.m., everybody who was anybody, and then some, assembled on the neatly manicured green lawn that fronted the Queen Anne-styled Marlborough Hotel. Dan Hennigan from the *Atlantic City Press* was doing double duty as reporter and photographer and correspondent for the Associated Press that Saturday. Gin had lured him with details of an intensely personal rivalry billed as "Ruth Versus Rockne".

With Mayor Walker acting as his second and firmly holding his index finger down on the football to hold it steady, at high noon precisely Babe took a couple of running steps and swung his hefty right leg at the brown oval. The ball went off the side of his black-and-white dress shoe and ended up in the boughs of a black pine tree about twenty yards away in the landscape that fronted the Marlborough's front porch.

A polite round of applause went up from the crowd that filled Ohio Avenue and lined the Boardwalk rail overlooking the lawn.

Knute then stepped onto the lawn, turned to face the crowds and in a loud voice announced he would kick his ball home in the direction of Indiana Avenue. Jack Dempsey performed the duty of second, bending down to steady the football in its tee. Knute laced up a pair of well-worn football shoes he always carried in his suitcase for good luck, took a running lead at the ball and punted it a good fifty yards north in the direction of Indiana. Cheers erupted from the crowds. Dan Hennigan was literally have a field day, snapping away with his new Fairchild camera, switching to his Zeiss Ikon for close-ups of the athletes.

A roar of laughter and cheers of approval erupted from the crowd as the Babe pulled out his money clip and peeled off ten one-hundred dollar bills, handing them one at a time to Knute. Knute stuck out his right hand and thanked Babe, and then turned the money over to Barry O'Connor.

"Here, you'll need to show this on your chapter's ledger for the South Bend office. Job well done. Congratulations!"

It was Kitty's last hours in Atlantic City. Come Sunday morning the families would be returning to the Oranges. Jimmy Sykes had left word for to rendez-vous on Ohio Avenue at 5 p.m. Once there, they observed the hotel's kitchen staff loading up a limousine with wicker picnic baskets, covered platters, and in the trunk, insulated crates filled with ice. Next, everyone climbed in and the chauffeur drove them to Gardner's Basin.

Once there, Jimmy introduced everyone to Captain Hank, the pony-tailed owner-operator of *Miss Atlantic City*, a spacious fifty-eight white cedar speed boat made by Elco Motor Yacht of Bayonne. It sat sixteen people with ease, handily accommodating all the food and crates of ice from the Blenheim's kitchen.

At five-thirty, the *Miss Atlantic City* cleared the mouth of Absecon Inlet and turned to starboard to parallel the coast, past the famous piers and hotels that were now familiar sights to Kitty. Captain Hank moved the throttles forward and the big Packard marine engine roared to life in a burst of spray. But instead of the usual itinerary along the island's beachfront, Captain Hank piloted east and out to sea.

"Hey, Jimmy, are we going to Europe for dinner?" Frank yelled forward to the pilot house where Jimmy stood next to Captain Hank. Everyone laughed, while Kitty began to chuckle to herself. She recalled Al Capone's suggestion that she take at least one trip out to sea to experience the rum-running business.

About ten miles east, the *Miss Atlantic City* ran into a curtain of heavy sea mist, a weather condition brought about from the collision of the sun-warmed air and the ocean's cool May waters. Captain Hank slowed his speed boat and put on its running lights as they ran at a dead slow through the watery curtain.

"Faint light off the starboard bow," Pete called out.

As everyone watched, the ghostly outline of a two-masted sailing ship appeared. From out of the watery dimness, a loud voice called out, "Boat ahoy!"

Jimmy Sykes cupped his hands and shouted back, "Greeks bearing gifts, Captain Ted."

As the mist gradually evaporated, the passengers on board the *Miss Atlantic City* saw an old ship swaying gently at her mooring. They also couldn't help but notice the armed men lined along her gunwales. The battered name plate on the stern proclaimed *That's My Hon* Bimini, Bahamas.

Swinging in under the lee of the schooner, the speed boat coasted closer in neutral, the sound of weathered rigging audible over the low growl of the engine. A tall figure appeared on the fantail, sporting a panama hat, denim shirt, and a dark leather jacket over weathered khakis. He waved his arm and three more men appeared at the rail, training Tommy guns on the guests below.

Balancing himself against the relentless motion of the waves,

Jimmy Sykes called "Permission to come aboard."

The man whose face showed a lifetime at sea stared down at the visitors for a moment. Then a slight grin spread across his face. "Permission granted."

Captain Ted turned around and barked a brief order and his men took the lines and tied off the *Miss Atlantic City* at the starboard waist and then helped its passengers board the ship. Next came up the cargo from the Blenheim Hotel.

Introductions were exchanged. Impressed to meet Kitty Dodd, Captain Ted gave her a tour of the hold of his ship. More than a thousand cases of spirits that included Haig & Haig Scotch, Bacardi Rum, Seagram's V.O., Holland Gin, and French wine filled the space.

"Business has been good?" Kitty asked.

"Extremely good, but not as safe after Bill McCoy was caught in '23," he replied. "It's much more cutthroat among competitors out here in the twelve-mile limit. And after McCoy's arrest, Treasury and the Coasties have been unpredictable about who they arrest."

"Will you be at it for much longer?" Kitty pressed on.

"The best thing that could happen is if Washington repeals Prohibition," Captain Ted responded. "Everybody goes legit and they let supply-and-demand sort itself out naturally. The best place to be in is distribution. You don't want to be making the stuff, Kitty. The islanders and the Europeans have been at it longer than you've drawn breath. It takes too much money. The greater profits are closer to the customer."

Kitty nodded. "Thank you, Ted, for your wisdom."

"You welcome, ma'm."

On deck, Kitty and Captain Ted joined the dinner that was spread out like a feast for knaves and kings, alike. Cooked lobster, grilled steak, platters of fresh produce from Atlantic City's outlying farms, and lots of newly chilled beer thanks to the crates of ice supplied by the Blenheim. Kitty sat down next to Doris.

"He is so handsome," Doris whispered to her grandmother. "He looks like Errol Flynn."

Kitty whispered back, "Captain Ted is a handsome rascal, alright. All he needs is an eye patch and a parrot!"

With the setting sun lighting up the clouds on the eastern horizon, the men began exchanging stories of the sea. Pete and Frank told of the ports of call they had made in Europe during the war. Jimmy Sykes and Jim Ryan told of their maritime exploits at home.

"Who knew then that the Coast Guard's surveillance tactics would be used against fellow Americans in this thing called Prohibition," Jimmy said.

"You know, on the day when we've completely emptied the hull and the Coasties try for a raid, we taunt them in song," Captain Ted told his new friends.

Instantly Frank wanted to know which ditties.

" 'What Do You Do With a Drunken Sailor' is a favorite," he chuckled. "And, 'How Dry I Am' never fails to frustrate the hell out of them."

Everyone laughed, and the conversation continued around the make-shift table set up in the middle of the deck. Kitty found her thoughts drifting away from the party. To the east, across the ocean, lay her homeland, Ireland. To the west lay America, her chosen home where liberty and the pursuit of happiness were written into the young nation's Declaration of Independence.

I've seen both sides that life has to offer: the hard life, chaffing against artificial limits, resorting to illegal acts just to scrape by. Now these last six days I've seen the other side of life where people live out in the open with their wealth. And they live well; with their own bathrooms and modern kitchens and garages for their cars. I've come along way since Cork and the days of making potcheen. The legacy I give my family has to be a legitimate one.

The sounds of approaching boats brought Kitty back to the present. In the twilight, Kitty saw boat after boat approaching the anchored ship where the crew had resume their positions at the gunwales, Tommy guns at the ready.

The families watched as burlap bags filled with cases of liquor were loaded onto the waiting boats only after Captain Ted took each buyer's cash. When there were no more arrivals Kitty found Captain Ted, Captain Hank and Jimmy Sykes conferring at the rail, looking at their watches, and nodding to each other. Two sailors hoisted three green lanterns up to the top of the main mast. Kitty thought to herself, *Here it comes, whatever it is.*

The families thanked Captain Ted and his crew for their hospitality as they re-boarded the *Miss Atlantic City.* Captain Hank put the speed boat in gear, taking the craft slowly past the multitude of smaller boats rolling gently to the Atlantic swells, many calling out a greeting to them in the darkness as they passed.

As they rounded the bow of the last ship, Captain Hank slowly advanced the throttle. Standing next to him, Jimmy Sykes scanned the western waters with binoculars. With no running lights on, they continued toward shore, increasing the boat's speed slowly as the craft followed a somewhat erratic course, first to starboard and then to port as Jimmy continued scanning the dark sea, whispering coordinates to Captain Hank.

Suddenly, loud enough for everyone to hear, Jimmy shouted "There they are! Two points off the starboard bow."

Kitty, Doris, Lil and Mary Monteverdi were startled as the *Miss Atlantic City*'s twin 440 horse-powered Packard engine roared to life.

"Everybody, hold on to your hats!" Jimmy yelled.

The big fifty-eight-footer lifted on to its plane and increased its already alarming speed. Their surprise turned to anxiety when a white star shell burst in the night sky above them and turned night into day as the bright light drifted slowly down on its parachute. Then, from their port side came a search light, the beam almost lost in the glare of the descending flare.

"Coast Guard boat swinging towards our stern," Pete pointed.

Jimmy looked and smiled.

How odd, Kitty thought. No, wait a minute. When they got off That's My Hon they brought nothing with them; not the Blenheim's picnic baskets, the empty ice crates. Why, they hadn't even brought any souvenir products from Captain Ted's floating liquor store.

The flair hit the sea and flickered out, but the ten-foot search beam held them, momentarily. Captain Hank turned the helm, trying to loose the accusing light. But again it found them. And when it did, three thunderous reports got their undivided attention. Three tall water columns grew out of the sea, a hundred yards off the bow.

"Jesus Christ, they're shooting at us!" Mary Monteverdi cried out in an uncharacteristic oath.

Captain Hank pulled the speed down slowly, switching on his boat's running lights as it came to a dead stop in the ocean waters. The Coast Guard cutter's lights raked the *Miss Atlantic City* as the vessel pulled up to its lee side. Her passengers shielded their eyes from the harsh glare. A metallic voice called out through a brass speaking trumpet: "Prepare to be boarded. Everyone keep you hands where we can see them."

As the seventy-five foot Coast Guard cutter eased along the fifty-eight-foot Elco Motor Yacht, the search light beam was lifted higher, but still throwing light on the scene.

Now able to see, Kitty saw uniformed men pointing Tommy

guns down on them. Another uniformed sailor aimed a large deck gun at them. Obediently, Kitty, Doris, Lil, Mary and even John Monteverdi, Jim and Frank and Pete all raised their hands high over their heads. Captain Hank and Jimmy Sykes did not.

Kitty leaned over to Doris and whispered "I have never seen so many men holding machine guns, Doris. Why don't you try and get their autographs?"

As the hemp fenders from the two boats gently touched, several Coast Guard officers jumped down and tied the ships together. Two more guards covered the passengers with their machine guns. As the boarding officers began their search, Captain Ian Macgregor called down, "Out for an evening cruise, are you Hank? You're a little off course. You might have chosen a less conspicuous boat for an evening run."

Just then a man in a suit and tie, a pair of winged shoes on his feet, jumped down on the white cedar gunwales, now slick with ocean spray, and began to slip. He wind-milled his arms to keep his balance. An alert sailor at the rail grabbed him by the forearm to steady him. As he regained his dignity, he took out a 38-caliber Smith & Wesson snub-nosed pistol in his left hand and in his right flashed a badge that read: U.S. Revenue Service, United States Department of the Treasury.

"I am government agent Jock Sanders and…." He got no further as he stared at the passengers.

"YOU!" He looked from face to face at Kitty Dodd and her sons and daughter who were looking back at him with a similar look of astonishment.

Slowly Jock's look of surprise turned into a smirk and he started to chortle.

"Well, well, isn't this the cat's ass. And, it isn't even my birthday."

He turned to Captain Macgregor who was standing on the deck of the cutter just above them watching everything.

"Captain, this is your lucky day. We've just captured the notorious Dodd gang from North Jersey. We got them red-handed, coming in from Rum Row. I have been trying to catch them for years and here they fall right into my hands with a boatload of booze! WOW! This is delicious indeed."

In the moment of silence as Ian Macgregor tried to absorb what the preening government agent was saying, Kitty put down her arms and began to titter. It turned into a chuckle, and before she could stop herself the mirth that had been hidden inside of her burst out into full-blown laughter. Still laughing, she fell backwards into her cushioned seat. Now she understood why all the rum runners had not departed after being loaded from *That's My Hon.* This so-called party in her honor was really a clever ploy. Kitty was the guest of honor, all right, but she was also the runners' decoy.

As his crew of investigating officers reboarded their vessel, Captain Macgregor noted that each held up empty palms, indicating they found nothing in their search.

"Your dangerous gang here doesn't seem to be carrying any contraband Agent Sanders," said Captain Macgregor. White was turning out to be a real pain in the ass, foisted on him by headquarters who ordered Ian to teach him the ins and outs of interdiction. In reality, HQ just wanted to get rid of the self-righteous, bumbling functionary.

"But, but, there must be… they have it hidden somewhere." A look of desperation replaced White's self-satisfied smirk. Frantically he started re-opening hatches and doors to compartments that had already been searched by the Coast Guard.

Silent up to now, a bored look deliberately fixed on his face,

Jimmy Sykes lit up a Chesterfield. "Captain Macgregor, may I introduce you to my friends and guests. This is Jim Ryan, my Coast Guard shipmate during the war."

Ian Macgregor doffed a casual salute as Jimmy made the round of introductions, saving Kitty for last.

Summoning her best Irish brogue and showing her winning smile, Kitty teasingly asked, "Captain Macgregor, is that a Glasgow accent I detect?"

Ian smiled broadly. He was deeply impressed with the family matriarch who seemed perfectly at ease as though search and seizure and getting shot at happened all the time in her worldly affairs.

Laying on a thick Scottish bur that he rarely used, he responded, "Aye, 'tis that my fair Colleen from County Cork?"

Kitty beamed. "You've a good ear yourself my good captain."

As they smiled at each other, they were interrupted by a now distraught and disheveled Jock Sanders who emerged from the engine hatch with his suit smeared with grease and oil, a sleeve torn, and his hair mused and hanging over his face.

"They're up to no good!" he shouted in a harsh, frustrated voice. "They must have dumped the cargo overboard."

"We came right up their wake, Agent Sanders, and didn't see any sign of it."

"But I tell you they're all criminals! They consort with known convicts. While here in Atlantic City they met with Al Capone!"

Fed up with Agent Sanders and his increasingly bizarre behavior, Captain Macgregor shook his head. He then smiled at Kitty and asked "Is that true, Kitty Dodd from County Cork?"

Before Kitty could answer, the night air started to fill with the sounds of engines. First a buzz. Then a whine. Then a full-throttled high-pitched cacophony of mechanized sound that swelled with the waves.

Captain Macgregor ran back to the landward rail and yelled, "Untie the lines on their boat and everyone back on board, on the double!"

Just as the captain called for "full speed" to the quartermaster in the wheel house, Jimmy Sykes shouted, "Hey Ian. You're forgetting something."

As the cutter started to pull away, Jimmy pointed to a dazed Agent Sanders, who was still on their boat.

"Jesus Christ," groaned Macgregor. "Reverse engines, helm, hard at starboard, engines dead slow, hands stand by to re-board that asshole."

Silently he asked: *Why me, God?*

It took several more minutes to bring the two ships back together again.

"No mooring lines, just hold us off until he's back on our deck," the captain ordered. "Sanders, get back aboard now!"

The beleaguered Treasury agent seemed to come to his senses. He moved to the rail and stepped on a seat to gain purchase on the gunwale. As he stepped forward, his leather-soled dress shoe slipped, and he started to fall forward. His flailing arms reached for the upper rail and missed. As he grasped the bottom rail, Agent Sanders found himself spread-eagle over the big hemp fender on the side of the cutter. Before anyone could grab him, the two hulls, gently came together again and pressed again his testicles.

A collective "Ouch!" came from the ladies. All the men on board both boats instantly covered their crotches.

"Oh my, that must hurt," Lil said with a straight face.

A Coast Guard sailor pulled a now screaming agent, not too gently, over the cutter's rail, and he curled into a fetal position with his hands between his legs, mouthing swear words, sotto voce.

The occupants of both ships barely held their laughter.

Kitty stood up and in her best Irish accent advised Agent Sanders, "Jock, take some care and mind the gap now."

The occupants of the two ships roared with laughter. The earlier sound of three dozen rum runners making their way into the porous inlets of New Jersey's crenellated coastline couldn't be heard any more, and Captain Macgregor knew he had been snookered by these charming people. He laughed the loudest.

They would not catch any rum runners this night, but it wasn't a total loss either. Ian Macgregor met some nice people and he watched Agent Sanders get his nuts cracked. No, not a bad night after all.

The Blenheim's limousine brought everyone back to the hotel. Jimmy Sykes promised to join them in the morning for a farewell breakfast. As the men debated whether or not to find one last midnight poker game to cap their Saturday celebration, Kitty urged the ladies to call it a night and return to the Wizard's Roost. For herself, however, she wanted one last adventure and made her way through the hotel lobby onto the Boardwalk, and turned right. Just past the Hotel Shelburne she found what she was looking for. Kitty opened the glass door and stepped inside the room softly lit in a pink light. Madame Zelda sat at the round table in the center of the patchouli-scented chamber that was hung in draperies, giving it the appearance of a tent on the sand. The woman, older than Kitty, nodded.

"How nice to see you return."

Kitty sat down.

"You want to know about your future."

It wasn't a question as much as it was a statement of fact. Kitty nodded.

Madame Zelda extended her hands across the table and

Kitty placed hers inside the dry, warm clasp of the woman from Transylvania. Both women closed their eyes.

"Life will get better. It's not that it's bad now. But there will be a bigger house with a porch and a business free from any interference."

Madame Zelda gently squeezed Kitty's hands. "You will have no worries."

A long moment passed.

"There will be more grandchildren. A boy and a girl. Not from the mother who gave you a granddaughter. But one of your other children."

Kitty's eyes flew open.

Madame Zelda pressed Kitty hands again and Kitty closed her eyes.

"They are already in your heart. Your Irish spirit will live on."

THE END

Postscript

On December 5, 1933, the 21st Amendment to the U.S. Constitution repealed the 18th. The so-called noble experiment to end public consumption of alcoholic was over. That day, my father, Frank, and Uncle Pete were issued Liquor License #1 in the City of Orange for an address on New Street. I was told they were able to open a fully stocked and furnished bar on Tuesday by merely taking the plywood panels off the windows and hanging up a neon sign that simply read: Dodd's Tavern. It was The Place you've just finished reading about: Same old, same old; only now it was legal! Later they would move the bar to Main Street and then to Center Street where I would eventually take the reins of the family business.

Sometime after Repeal, the Internal Revenue Service estimated that millions of stills had operated with impunity during the thirteen long years of Prohibition. Large and small-scale production, whether for home consumption or for sale or trade, had outpaced the demand for the more expensive, commercially made foreign liquor smuggled in by rum runners.

To be sure, at any one time, there were fewer than two thousand revenue agents to cover the whole country, its borders and coasts. Agents were paid an average of two thousand dollars a year. Many would be seduced by protection money while many more just stopped trying as case after case was dismissed or thrown out of the court for more pressing complaints.

The combined efforts of all law enforcement agencies reduced less than five percent of the illegal industry, or about the same percentage of our current War on Drugs which has been waged for more than forty years!

Congress would have done better had it listened to Martin Behrman, a long-time mayor of New Orleans, who famously said of that other immoral vice, prostitution, and attempts to outlaw it:

"You can make it illegal, but you can't make it unpopular."

LaVergne, TN USA
14 September 2009
157835LV00003B/25/P